# HOLLY

## ALSO BY JUDE DEVERAUX

*The Velvet Promise*
*Highland Velvet*
*Velvet Song*
*Velvet Angel*
*Sweetbriar*
*Counterfeit Lady*
*Lost Lady*
*River Lady*
*Twin of Fire*
*Twin of Ice*
*The Temptress*
*The Raider*
*The Princess*
*The Awakening*
*The Maiden*
*The Taming*
*The Conquest*
*A Knight in Shining Armor*
*Wishes*
*Mountain Laurel*
*The Duchess*
*Eternity*
*Sweet Liar*
*The Invitation*
*Remembrance*
*The Heiress*
*Legend*
*An Angel for Emily*
*The Blessing*
*High Tide*
*Temptation*
*The Summerhouse*
*The Mulberry Tree*
*Forever. . .*
*Wild Orchids*
*Forever and Always*

# JUDE DEVERAUX

## HOLLY

**ATRIA** BOOKS

New York London Toronto Sydney Singapore

**ATRIA** BOOKS
1230 Avenue of the Americas
New York, NY 10020

This book is a work of fiction. Names, characters, places and
incidents are products of the author's imagination or are used
fictitiously. Any resemblance to actual events or locales or persons,
living or dead, is entirely coincidental.

# HOLLY

# Prologue

"ARE YOU SURE YOU WANTA DO THIS, DOC?" CARL asked, looking across to the driver's seat at Dr. Nicholas Taggert. "My brother's cabin is a wreck and the only transportation there is his truck, and it isn't street legal so you can't drive it."

Nick looked in his left mirror, signaled, then moved Carl's car into the fast lane. "I told you that all I need is a place to get away to for a few days, and my cousin is going to pick me up. You said there's a grocery within walking distance so I won't need a vehicle for the three days I'm alone there."

"It's just a mom-and-pop store. No caviar or anything." When Nick didn't smile, Carl knew his joke had fallen flat. "Sorry about your girl," he mumbled.

"Over and done with," Nick said tightly, letting it be known that Stephanie Benning was not something he was going to discuss.

Carl looked out the window at the beautiful Smokey Mountain scenery, but he was so nervous he could hardly sit still. What was he, an ambulance driver, doing in a car with a big-deal doctor like Nicholas Taggert? Why hadn't Dr. Nick asked one of the doctors at the clinic if they knew of a cabin to rent? They could have found him a place on five acres, near a movie theater and something called a "bistro."

Carl couldn't figure out why Dr. Nick wanted to stay in a derelict cabin, but he did know why the man wanted to hide out: Stephanie Benning, ol' Doc Benning's youngest—and meanest—daughter.

About nine months ago, long-legged, long-haired Stephanie had come back from some place with a French name, the ink still wet on her divorce papers, taken one look at Dr. Nick Taggert's movie-star good looks, and gone after him like there was no tomorrow. Of course everyone in the office knew that she wasn't after his looks. Her last husband had been the clone of a toad. She knew that Dr. Nick was from money—real money. Big money. He didn't know anyone in the office knew about his family's worth, but they did. Ten minutes on the Internet and the news was out.

More of a secret was what Stephanie Benning was really like. Only the locals in the clinic knew that she'd been a selfish, hateful child and she hadn't changed as she got older. Somehow, she'd managed to fool Dr. Nick for eight whole months before he broke up with her.

Of course Stephanie told everyone in her father's clinic that she'd been the one to break it off. She'd said that Dr. Taggert had used her, then thrown her away like an old handbag. She'd wept so prettily that everyone except the locals believed her. She'd even made a big deal about the yellow diamond Dr. Nick had given her because he'd asked for it back. She'd whined that no gentleman would demand the return of jewels given to a lady.

One of the women in the office said the rock was worth at least a million and belonged to Dr. Nick's family.

"I notice she kept that big dinner ring he gave her," Lucy in reception had snipped.

"And the sapphire earrings," someone else said.

"And the pearl necklace."

"All she had to give back was that big yellow diamond and the key to the ball and chain she'd clamped around him."

Everyone had fallen over in laughter.

But the physicians on the staff at the Benning Clinic had believed everything Stephanie had said about Dr. Nick. Overnight, words like "gentleman," "honor" and "integrity," were overheard—as though Nick Taggert didn't have these qualities.

The locals had tried to defend him, but they couldn't say much. After all, Stephanie's father signed their paychecks.

One of the women tried to get Dr. Nick to defend himself and tell the truth about what Stephanie was like. They didn't know the details of the breakup, but they were sure he'd found out that all she wanted was his money. But Dr. Nick wouldn't defend himself. He bore the looks from the other doctors and the whispered comments without flinching. Even when Stephanie threw one of her spoiled-brat tantrums in front of the entire staff and the waiting patients, he still didn't defend himself.

The locals were split down the middle about his silence. Half said he was an idiot and the other half said he was a hero out of a storybook.

So, three nights ago, when Carl had returned from a late run and Dr. Nick had been alone in his office, Carl hadn't been shocked when Dr. Nick asked if he knew of a cabin to rent, a place to get away for a few days. But a cabin that would suit the likes of a man with the doctor's pedigree was out of Carl's league.

Carl had just smiled. "The only place I know of is my brother Leon's house. It's fallin' down enough that you could call it a cabin, and it *is* on a lake."

"Sounds great. When will your brother be away so I can rent it?"

"He'll be gone for about twelve more years," Carl said, still smiling. "If he behaves himself, that is. Look, Doc, I was just kidding. You do *not* want to rent Leon's place. It's horrible. The house is a pigsty and it's got a big barn that looks like it's gonna fall down any minute. The truth is, atomic bombs wouldn't hurt that barn, but that's neither here nor there.

Now, across the lake, just on the other side, are some really nice houses. I bet if you called a realtor–"

"How far from here is your brother's cabin?"

"A couple of hours. But, Doc–"

"Is it vacant now? Is it furnished?"

"Sort of," Carl said, then got louder, firmer. He needed to stop this *now*. "You can*not* rent Leon's place, Doc, it's awful. My brother has only one interest in his life and that's his truck. He dedicated every penny he could earn, steal, or con somebody out of to that truck. He's in prison now because he robbed three gas stations just so he could buy a spare transmission and a transfer case."

Carl could see that Dr. Nick wasn't listening to him.

"Does the roof leak?"

"No," Carl said patiently. "I look after the place enough that the roof doesn't leak, and I cleaned it up enough that the rats don't tear down the walls to get at the food Leon left lyin' around. Doc!" he said emphatically. "You can't think of stayin' in that house."

Dr. Nick leaned back in his chair and narrowed his eyes at Carl. "Why not? Do you think I'm too much of a priss to get my hands dirty in a house like your brother's?"

Carl had to smile at the word "priss." In the five years Dr. Nick had been at the Benning Clinic, he'd never heard the man use foul language. He'd always been fair and honest to everyone, but, until Stephanie, he'd never been close to any of them, not doctors or staff. He was a good doctor and the only times Carl or anyone else had seen Dr. Nick get angry was when a patient wasn't getting the best of service.

In the end, no matter what Carl said, Nick Taggert had overridden him, and now they were driving through the mountains to Leon's cabin.

As they drove up the weed-infested driveway, Carl relaxed. There was no way anyone on earth would want to stay in this place unless he had to. It was almost with triumph that Carl said, "Watch out for snakes," as soon as they stepped into the waist-high weeds that surrounded the old house.

He walked behind Dr. Nick as he battled through the weeds to the front steps of the house, then up to the porch. There was no reason to lock the house; who'd want to go inside it?

In the living room were three pieces of furniture Leon had found at the dump, the stuffing coming out of the arms. The two end tables, the coffee table, and both lamps were made of beer cans welded together. The dining room had an old table, hidden somewhere under Leon's collection of a couple of thousand old car magazines. The kitchen was the worst, with cracked dishes on the floor, magazines with curled pages, dented aluminum pots, and mouse droppings everywhere. At the back of the house was the bedroom, with an old, stained mattress and a jumble of torn, dirty sheets at the bottom of a closet.

"See what I mean?" Carl said when they were outside on the back porch. In front of them stretched the lake, crystal clear and beautiful. Across the pristine surface, on the other side, were gorgeous houses, each house painted a different color, with a matching boat dock. Some people even had boats painted to match their houses and docks.

When Leon had been arrested, Carl had wanted to sell the lake house to pay for a good lawyer, but Leon had refused. He said that someday the developers would want his place and Leon would make them pay.

"I bet you can get one of those houses over there," Carl said, nodding across the lake.

Nick was leaning on the porch rail and looking across the water. "Lavender," he said.

"What?"

"I don't see a lavender house. There are three shades of pink, but little in the lavender family. What if I paint this house lavender, build a matching boat dock, and get a sailboat with bright purple sails?"

It took Carl moments to realize that Nick was kidding. Laughing, Carl slapped him on the back. "As long as you don't touch the truck, you can do whatever you want to to the place."

Nick stood up and stretched, and Carl could see that, in a way, the doc fit with this place. There was something old world about the man that suited this half-overgrown old house.

Abruptly, all Carl's nervousness left him. The doc would do all right here.

"So where's this infamous truck?" Nick said, stepping back for Carl to lead the way.

Carl took the set of keys out of his pocket as he kicked weeds aside. When Leon had bought the place years ago, Carl had tried to get him to tear down the old barn. He'd said Leon should build a new, secure building of concrete blocks to use for his garage.

"I plan to," Leon said, but Carl hadn't known what he meant. Leon had built a new building inside the barn, camouflaging it so no one would guess what was inside.

Carl unlocked the old barn door, then used a code to unlock the inner steel door. If Dr. Nick was surprised, he didn't show it. When Carl slid the heavy steel door back, the lights inside the garage went on. Carl gave a little smile when, behind him, he heard Dr. Nick gasp. It was an enormous, windowless room, spotlessly clean, with two smaller glass-walled rooms inside, one outfitted with a bath and a full kitchen.

In the main room a two-ton overhead electric hoist system and a bead blasting system sat near a Hollander drill press, a band saw, a puller set, an air compressor, and a parts washer. There were several tall metal cabinets in deep red full of Hollander tools. Always the best for Leon.

In the middle of the room, on a concrete floor that even

after six months barely showed any dust, was the truck. The Truck.

Dr. Nick stepped into the shop and stood a few feet back from the truck, looking at it with wide eyes.

"Ever see anything like it?"

"Never," Nick answered. "What, exactly *is* it?"

Carl knew that to the uninitiated the truck looked bizarre. It was a 1978 Chevy half-ton body, with a Chrysler V-10 engine. Nearly everything inside the truck had been removed and replaced by something better, and more expensive, and bigger. As a result, every square inch was filled with machinery.

Since Carl had spent too many weekends helping his brother, he knew a lot about what had been done to the truck, and while Dr. Nick listened in appreciative silence, Carl gave him the full rundown, explaining why the bed of the truck was filled with machines and pipes. When Carl quit talking—not that he'd finished—he looked at Dr. Nick, who was blinking at the truck as though trying to comprehend it.

"So how fast does it go?"

"One fifty, easy. But this thing will climb, too. It's for off-road racing."

"Legally?"

"Leon never did understand the difference between legal and illegal."

Nick put out his hand and gingerly touched the side of the truck. "I've never been a lover of machinery, but I envy your brother's passion. He loved something so much that he risked everything for it."

"I guess you could look at it like that. I can tell you that none of his family did. Look, Doc–" he began, but Nick put up his hand.

"I'd be proud to take the place for the next few days. I like it here."

"Even the kitchen?"

"Which one?" Nick said, looking toward the glassed-in office.

Suddenly, Carl's face turned white. "You mean you'd stay in *here?* In Leon's garage?"

"I won't hurt . . . it," Nick said, looking at the truck. "I certainly don't plan to drive it."

Carl hadn't thought of anyone staying in Leon's garage, and for a moment he had a vision of his brother escaping prison and coming after him. In Leon's mind, the blood bond wasn't nearly as strong as what he felt for his truck.

"I, uh, I . . ." Carl stuttered.

Nick looked at his watch. "Aren't you on shift in about two and a half hours?"

"I . . ."

"Go on!" Nick said. "Leave me here alone with the truck and I'll take care of it. I'm just going to do some fishing and I'll sleep in here. That house is ..." Words seemed to fail him when attempting to describe the house.

"I ..." Carl said again, then the next moment Nick's hands were on his shoulders and he was being pushed out of the garage and escorted back to his car. Nick took the keys, the paper with the code to the garage alarm system on it, and his bags from the back, and the next thing Carl knew he'd started the engine and was driving away.

"Leon is gonna kill me," he said all the way back to the clinic.

# Chapter One

HOLLY FELT AS THOUGH SHE'D PULLED OFF THE coup of her life—and by Christmas it would all be settled. After many calls, letters, emails, and promises, she'd finally persuaded her parents to buy Spring Hill Plantation just outside beautiful, historic Edenton in eastern North Carolina. Of course, it hadn't hurt that her stepsister, Taylor, was going to marry a man who lived there.

Now, she was in the little grocery store that was two miles down the road from the ghastly house her parents had rented last year and she was trying to find something to eat that didn't have a thousand calories a bite. She'd recently lost eleven pounds and she didn't want to put it back on. Facing a summer near her skinny, beautiful stepsister had made her quit eating and go to the gym four nights a week.

And of course there was the prospect of seeing Lorrie again, she thought. For a moment her eyes glazed over as she remembered him. She was no longer seeing the store, but instead, saw the river and the dock and Lorrie. She'd been thirteen that summer and Lorrie had been sixteen—a tall, lean, bronzed young man, with golden hair and brown eyes.

That summer had started out horribly. Her parents nearly always rented a house somewhere for the summer, but until that year the houses had been in communities where their two daughters could swim and meet other people their own age.

But that summer a friend of her father's had offered them the free use of his beautifully restored old house, built in 1778, located on a river, and set in the midst of four and a half acres of old trees and pretty flower gardens.

Holly had hated the place at first sight. Its isolation, the remoteness, had made her want to scream. In an instant she'd envisioned a summer in a hell of loneliness. Taylor was old enough to drive so she'd be going to nearby Edenton and joining the real world.

But what am I to do here the whole summer? she thought, near to tears. Catch tadpoles? Sit by the river and watch the turtles come up for air? It wasn't what a pubescent girl wanted to do.

She'd tried to persuade her parents that they absolutely, positively could *not* force her to stay in that horrible place for an entire summer. They'd just smiled, then answered the always-ringing telephone.

For the first week, Holly had been so bored she thought she might lose her mind. Her parents had already left to fly to London, and Taylor had met a young man. Holly had been left in the charge of a woman who was at least as old as the house and who did little except sleep in the padded swing on the back porch.

It was at the beginning of the second week that Holly had been sitting on the edge of the pier, her legs tucked up to her chest, and contemplating her family's regret if their youngest child ran away from home, when she heard an unusual noise. She looked up to see a rowboat coming toward her.

She had to blink, then rub her eyes and blink again to be sure she was seeing correctly. Coming toward her, his back to her, was a beautiful, shirtless young man. She couldn't see his face, but if the front of him was half as good as the back of him, he was an Adonis.

Holly had stood up, smoothed her shorts and T-shirt— wishing she weren't wearing her rattiest clothes—and waited.

When he reached her dock and turned, he was so beautiful that her breath nearly stopped.

"Hello," he'd said, throwing a rope at her feet. "I'm Laurence Beaumont and I'm your next-door neighbor. You want to tie that down?"

She had no idea what he meant. Tie what down?

"The rope," he said. "Tie it to the cleat."

It had taken her a moment to understand what he meant.

Cleat? Oh, yeah, the thing she used to scrape mud off her shoes. She picked up the rope and tied it in a very neat bow to the metal cleat, then looked over at the young man.

He looked at the cleat, then back at her, but he didn't laugh. Later, she wondered at that. What other sixteen-year-old would have looked at a boat rope tied into a bow and not howled with laughter?

But Lorrie hadn't laughed at her, not then, nor at any other time.

From that first moment, they'd been friends–kindred souls maybe, since they were so alike. Her name was Hollander, his was Laurence, but they were Holly and Lorrie to everyone. His family had lived in the same house since 1782 and two of his ancestors had signed the Declaration of Independence.

Holly had some big-shot ancestors on her father's side, and her father himself had been an ambassador to three different countries. "He knows everybody and talks to each one every day on the phone," she'd said under the breath.

Lorrie had laughed. "My old man makes deals all day."

"What about your mother?"

"Died when I was three."

Holly felt as though she'd been hit in the stomach. Her mother had died when she was one. When she told Lorrie, he sat down on the dock and they began to compare notes of their lives in earnest.

Both their fathers had been raised in impoverished gentility, with fabulous educations and old-world family names. Both fathers had married heiresses who'd died young. Both men had remarried women with no money. The difference was that Holly's stepmother, Marguerite, was a sort of financial genius, while Lorrie's stepmother's main talent was in spending. Holly's mother's fortune, from Hollander Tools, had increased, while Lorrie's mother's fortune had long ago disappeared.

"All I have left is the title to the falling-down old house and a few hundred acres," Lorrie had said cheerfully, looking at Holly. "What is it about you, kid, that's making me tell you my life story? I didn't tell my last three girlfriends this much."

Holly hadn't liked being called "kid," and she didn't like to think that this beautiful young man had ever had a girlfriend, but she took the compliment to her heart. "I guess we were just meant to be together," she said, willing him to take her away forever in his canoe.

Smiling, Lorrie tousled Holly's short, dark hair. "Maybe so, kid. Maybe you're what I need this summer. Hey! I'll race you to the other side of the river."

Holly wasn't a very good swimmer, but by the end of that summer she was, for she spent nearly every day with Lorrie. Although Lorrie had revealed lots of secrets about his past, she soon found out that he was close-mouthed about his current life. It was only through listening to the gossip her stepsister so loved that she knew Lorrie was hiding out that summer.

"The biggest snobs in eastern North Carolina," Taylor had said at dinner. She was talking about the Beaumont family. "They've lived here since George Washington surveyed the area and even have a few letters from him. But seventeen years ago, the family was broke, so Laurence Beaumont the second married some rich little heiress and she conveniently died three years after having Larry the third."

As always, Taylor had been oblivious to the emotions her careless words caused. Their father had also married an heiress who died young.

"Lorrie, not Larry," Holly said and immediately wished she could take the words back. Her father, her stepmother, and her stepsister paused to look at her in surprise.

"The cook works for them sometimes," she muttered, looking down at her food.

Taylor gave Holly a speculative look before returning to her gossip. Taylor was as gregarious as Holly was quiet. Taylor loved being in a crowd, while Holly wanted just a couple of girlfriends to pal around with.

Taylor had gone on to say that Lorrie—"silly nickname for a boy," she'd said—was supposed to have gone to some elegant summer camp, but at the last minute one of his father's stupid land deals fell through so there was no money. "The kid doesn't want any of his rich friends to know, so he's hiding out at his father's family's rotting old house. Have you seen him?"

It took Holly a moment to realize her stepsister was talking to her. "Who?" she asked, her heart fluttering wildly. She didn't want anyone to know she was spending most of her time alone with a sixteen-year-old boy. Even though all she was doing was helping Lorrie remove paint off the molding in the old house, she feared that if they knew, they'd stop her.

"She's been reading the classics, haven't you?" her father said, looking at his only child fondly. Taylor was his wife's daughter.

Holly looked at her plate and nodded.

Somehow she managed to keep her secret all summer. Her father and stepmother had flown in and out all that summer; Taylor had spent her time in Edenton, and the woman hired to baby-sit Holly couldn't have cared less where her charge spent the day.

It had been a magical summer of long, hot days spent with Lorrie. They'd constantly worked together on his family's plantation. His family had lived there since it was built before the American Revolutionary War, and Lorrie loved the place as much as his father hated it. One day while they were painting the dining room, Lorrie told her that his mother had married his father for his name and his home. She'd traded her fortune for the Beaumont history.

Lorrie's grandfather, shrewd in business, had blessed his daughter's marriage even though he saw what Laurence Beaumont was. However, before the marriage he'd made sure the plantation was given to his daughter's children so that her husband couldn't sell the place.

"I don't remember her," Lorrie said as she stroked butter-nut-colored paint onto the clean molding. "But I've been told she loved this house so much that she died for it." He said the last with bitterness. He told Holly that his mother had died giving birth to another child. She'd so wanted to have her baby born in the Beaumont house that, against the doctor's orders, she'd tried for a home birth. There were complications and both mother and child had died before the ambulance could get them to the hospital.

"Maybe your mother's death is why your father hates this place."

"Naw. He just loves Tiffany's ass more."

Tiffany was his father's third wife and Lorrie despised her. She'd made her husband buy her a new, modern house in Raleigh and they stayed there, rarely even visiting the old plantation.

Holly never asked Lorrie about the camp he was supposed to have gone to. In fact, she didn't ask him about anything that didn't have to do with the house. He took her around to the falling-down outbuildings and told her what they'd been used for. He talked of his dream of someday restoring every building and being "a gentleman farmer," he'd said, smiling.

"You can do it, Lorrie, I know you can."

He'd laughed and tousled her hair—the only way he ever touched her.

It had been an idyllic summer in spite of the fact that she spent ninety-nine percent of her waking hours and a hundred percent of her sleeping hours imagining Lorrie kissing her. She stared at his lips until she knew every little crease in them.

If Lorrie had any idea she had a crush on him he never let her know. At the end of the summer she had to go back to school—this one in Ireland—and Lorrie had a year of high school to finish.

When they'd said good-bye, he'd picked her up, twirled her around, and said she was the kid sister he'd never had. Holly'd looked at him and willed him to kiss her. He did, but only on the forehead, then he'd tousled her hair one last time before he got in his car and drove away.

She'd told him she'd write him and she did. For six months she wrote Lorrie long letters, pouring her heart out to him, telling him of spats at her boarding school and of any accomplishments she was proud of. The only time he'd written back was when she sent him a paper she'd written about Colonial architecture. Lorrie had sent her a postcard that said, "Good work, kid. L."

It was that summer with Lorrie that sent her on her career path. She decided to study architecture in college, but that soon changed to architectural history, then narrowed to American domestic architecture.

Over the years his lack of response made her stop sending him letters, but she never lost track of him. She followed his career after he graduated from law school, and she saw how he won nearly every case. She sent him a card of sympathy when she read that his father had shot himself after another bogus land deal had left him impoverished. She cried for three days after she read that Lorrie got married. But Lorrie's marriage had been good for her. It had made her stop living in a fantasy, take her nose out of the books, and begin looking at the men around her.

She'd grown up to look like her mother, who had won a couple of beauty pageants, so Holly had never had trouble getting men. Over the years she'd had a few love affairs, one serious, but she'd never given her heart away. She'd never told anyone about her summer with the boy next door, but she knew that no man had ever made her feel as Lorrie had. No man had made her feel as though she wanted to say, "Here's my life, take it. Do with me what you will."

When she turned twenty-one, she came into her inheritance. Millions. After two days of elation and buying new clothes, she decided she had to do something real with the money, something worthwhile. What interested her was the preservation of old houses, but at the same time she didn't want to become one of those rich women real preservationists put up with just for the money. She wanted to be treated as though she had a brain in her head, as though she knew

Federal from Colonial from Greek Revival. She decided to get her Ph.D. in American architecture.

When she turned twenty-four, her father had a mild heart attack and was told to stop jetting all over the world. While Holly was at the hospital, she'd flipped through a *Town & Country* magazine. It had been two years since she'd read anything outside her subject so she could barely comprehend the magazine. It was when she saw the name Laurence Beaumont III that her eyes began to focus. The article said that Mr. Beaumont had recently divorced and that he was going home to his plantation outside Edenton, North Carolina, to open a law office there.

Suddenly it was as though everything Holly had ever wanted was within her grasp. She knew she had the money to buy the house next to Lorrie's, but she also instinctively knew that he'd know exactly what she was up to. She'd learned that, to men, the chase was everything.

As soon as her father was well enough to leave the hospital, she started her campaign to get him—not her—to buy Spring Hill, the old house they'd stayed in when she was thirteen. The isolation would allow him the peace he needed, she said. Maybe he could buy a pedal boat and get his exercise by gliding down the river.

Holly felt guilty about it, but she then led her father into asking her to please spend the summer with them. When he had finally asked, she acted reluctant, until her father said, "If you can't, that's all right," then turned to his wife to change the subject.

Too loudly, Holly said that maybe the old house would be a good place for her to write her dissertation for her doctorate.

Her stepsister had looked at her so sharply that Holly'd had to hide her face. Her parents were so busy with their own lives that they didn't have time to examine the lives of their two daughters, but Taylor rarely missed anything.

"I think Holly has a good idea," Taylor said.

When Holly looked up, her stepsister's eyes were saying that she meant to find out what Holly was up to.

After that, everything seemed to fall into place. Taylor had returned to Edenton to check out the house, had re-met an old flame, and had, unexpectedly, become engaged. She was planning an enormous wedding to take place on Christmas Eve and Holly was to be her maid of honor.

Holly's secret was that she fantasized about making it a double wedding. She and Taylor would walk down the aisle together and join the men in their lives at the altar.

However, Taylor knew Holly was up to something. "I don't know what you are up to but I'll find out," Taylor had said, then she'd smiled and asked Holly to take over some tasks for her. When Holly protested that she didn't have time, Taylor said she'd strongly suggest to her parents that they *not* retire to the house outside Edenton. "They can stay in a hotel for the wedding. After all, after I'm married I plan to travel so there's no need on my part for our parents to live in Edenton. But if *you* want them to live there . . ."

"Blackmail," Holly had muttered more than once after her stepsister had dumped yet another unpleasant task on her.

One of Holly's jobs was to go to the house her parents had rented before her father's heart attack and oversee the movers. Dutifully, she had left her studies to go to an atrocious house in the Smokey Mountains to pack everything up. When she saw the pink and white house, with its matching boathouse, she was appalled. To her, any house built after 1840 wasn't worth living in.

So now she was in the little resort area around Lake Winona and waiting for the movers to show up. Everything in the house except for one bed had been boxed or crated and all that was needed now was to put it all on the truck. But the truck had broken down somewhere and they'd called to tell her they would be late, but that they'd be there for sure by 3:00 P.M.

Now, at noon, Holly was in the little general store near the house and trying to decide what to buy for dinner. She could get lunch at the little diner at the front of the store, but she'd cook dinner. She had a jar of pasta sauce in each hand and was trying to decide between the two when she looked over the counter into the dark blue eyes of an extraordinarily handsome man. He had black hair that swept across his forehead, rather like Superman's, and a full-lipped mouth set over a cleft chin.

"Oh!" Holly said, then ducked down to grab the jar of sauce she'd nearly dropped. When she stood up again, the man was gone. Turning, she saw him walk toward the glass doors. He was tall, lean, broad-shouldered, slim-hipped.

On the other hand, he had on paint-spattered old blue jeans and a torn T-shirt that said TRUCKERS LIVE IN HEAVEN. He's from the other side of the lake, she thought. The people who lived in the "real" houses.

She put the jars of pasta sauce back on the shelf and decided she'd grill some shrimp instead. Maybe she should go into town and get a bottle of wine or two. Just because she was alone was no reason to live on jarred pasta sauce, she told herself.

She took a seat at one of the three tables at the end of the store, and waited while the woman at the cash register finished with the customers before she took Holly's order. While she waited, she looked out the window. "He" was there, the beautiful man she'd just seen. There were several people in the graveled parking lot and three big motorcycles. "Hogs," she thought. That's what the big motorcycles were called and the women, with their over-bleached hair and sleeveless leather vests, were "biker chicks." At least she thought those were the correct terms. With her past, she was more likely to know the name of the Queen of Lanconia's best friend (Dolly) than motorcycle slang.

The woman at the register was still busy with customers so

Holly kept watching the scene outside. The man she'd seen–who she'd nicknamed "Heaven" because of his shirt–didn't seem to know the others in the group. He had a bag of groceries and seemed to want to be on his way, but the bikers kept blocking him.

Why? she wondered. As the big-bellied bikers talked to the man, the two women circled behind him, looking him up and down, then laughing and nudging each other. Holly smiled to herself. If she were with them, she'd be laughing, too. He was a gorgeous man!

"Honey, you don't want anything to do with the likes of him."

Startled, Holly looked up at the waitress. "I, uh . . ." she began, unsure of what to say.

"You're Ambassador Latham's daughter, right?"

Holly nodded. She was used to people knowing "who" she was.

"He's good to look at, but he's a friend of Leon Basham's, so you don't want to get involved. Besides, a girl as pretty as you are doesn't need his kind."

"I wasn't– I don't–" Holly said, frowning, but then couldn't resist asking, "Who's Leon Basham?"

"A thief, a liar, and a cheat," the waitress said. "He's one of those truck racers. They have these big, ugly trucks that they race up hills on the weekends. They take the things all over the country to race them."

"That doesn't sound so bad," Holly said. She couldn't stop glancing at the man. There was a way he carried himself, the way his shoulders stood back at attention, the way he looked the other people in the eyes, that intrigued her.

"Leon's different. He robbed half a dozen places in a fifty-mile radius of here before he got caught. He did odd jobs around the area to make enough to live on, but it wasn't enough to pay for that truck."

"What does this guy Leon have to do with *him?*" Holly nodded toward the scene outside. Now it looked as though the men were trying to get "Heaven" to ride one of their motorcycles.

"He's staying in Leon's place. You can't call that shack a house."

"Yeah, but he's got that barn," said a man who walked past them.

Holly saw the woman sneer and could tell that she hated her employer. He was dressed like the locals, in T-shirt and jeans, but the waitress was dressed like Holly: khaki trousers, cotton knit shirt with a collar, and a striped belt. Holly would have thought the woman was a college student with a summer job, except that she was probably in her early forties.

"My husband thinks it's noble to dedicate your life to a truck," she said in a tone of disgust.

Holly was just thinking that the two of them were certainly mismatched as a couple when their attention was caught by what was happening outside. One of the women took the groceries from Heaven, and the man put one long leg over a huge motorcycle.

The waitress put her hand on the table as she looked out the window. "It's a trick. It's a test. That machine is souped-up, so if he touches the gas petal he'll go flying off the back. They know he's living in Leon's house, so they want to see if he's worthy of having a key to the barn."

"What's so important about the barn?" Holly asked, never taking her eyes off the man. Was he about to be thrown into the gravel? Would he land on his beautiful face? On the other hand, maybe she'd have to administer CPR to him.

One of the biker men started to explain the controls, but Heaven pushed his hand away.

"He seems to know what he's doing," Holly said.

"He'd have to if Leon let him have a key," the woman's husband said. He'd moved to stand beside his wife, who turned on him.

"You know that Leon's in jail. Carl probably gave the man a key and Leon doesn't even know he has it."

"Carl's not stupid. He knows Leon would kill him if he did that."

"Over a key to a barn?" Holly asked.

"Yes!" the man and woman said in unison.

The three of them turned back to watch the man on the motorcycle.

"Five he falls," the woman said.

"Ten he makes it," Holly said before the man could speak. She didn't see the waitress frown at the back of her head.

As the bikers stood back, smiles on their faces, Heaven kick-started the machine—no electric ignition—and seconds later left the parking lot in a blaze of flying gravel, then hit the pavement at full speed.

For a moment the bikers looked chagrined, but as the seconds passed, they seemed to worry that he'd never return with the bike. If he was the thieving Leon's friend, had he stolen the motorcycle?

Several long minutes later, the man returned from a different direction and, again in a flurry of gravel, stopped the bike exactly where he'd taken off. Calmly, he dismounted and took his groceries from the woman who was still holding them.

"You owe her ten bucks," the man said to his wife, "and get her something to eat." He sauntered away, obviously pleased.

As the woman removed a ten-dollar bill from her apron, Holly said, "You don't have to pay me. It was all in fun."

"I pay my debts," she said tersely, and Holly knew she was angry at her husband. "Now, what can I get you? And before you ask, we have no pasta salad—or any kind of salad to speak of." Her voice was rising so her husband could hear. "All we have is pork. If we serve it, it has pork in it or on it. Even the chicken is fried in half bacon grease."

"A sandwich?" Holly said meekly, not wanting to be part of a domestic quarrel.

"I suggest a club sandwich," the waitress said loudly. "Even though it has ham and bacon on it."

"Okay," Holly said. "And a glass of unsweetened tea."

"Hear that, Ralph?" she yelled. "Here's one of the city people who does *not* want half a pound of sugar in her drink."

Holly was relieved when the waitress went away and she again looked at her watch. She'd planned to stay another night after the truck took the furniture away, but maybe she wouldn't. Maybe she'd leave this evening.

When the waitress brought her sandwich and tea, Holly willed her to go away, but she stood there until Holly looked up at her.

"Look," the woman said softly, then slid into the booth across the table. "I'm sorry for that outburst, sorry you were involved in it, but you remind me of myself at your age. You wouldn't think so to look at me now, but I used to look a lot like you." Leaning forward she glared at Holly. "And my husband looked a lot like that man you were lusting over."

"I wasn't—" Holly began, but decided to take a bite of sandwich instead of finishing the sentence.

"They're sometimes gorgeous when they're young."

"They?" Holly asked.

"You know, these local boys. Boys who are driving pickups by the time they're eleven; boys whose dads give them rifles for their ninth birthdays; boys who've never eaten anything that hasn't bedded down with a pig."

"Bedded . . . ? Oh," Holly said. *Those* boys. Forbidden boys. Boys who weren't the "right sort." Boys who grew up to be men like the one her stepmother had first married.

"I was like you and I fell in love with a beautiful young man who made love to me on the seat of his pickup. He told me he'd like to give me the moon for a mirror."

"That sounds sweet," Holly said.

"Yeah, and look where it got me." She gestured around the little grocery. Holly knew that the people on "her side" of the lake never ate at the diner. "The cholesterol content of the food would kill you in thirty seconds flat," her stepsister had said. It was true that Holly's club sandwich had about a quarter of a cup of mayonnaise on it and at least four slices of bacon and three slices of ham. It was delicious, but Holly figured she'd gain a pound from this one meal.

"So why don't you get out?" Holly said before she thought. She'd always been a practical person. Yeah, it had hurt that the boy she wanted didn't want her, but life went on. And, now, wasn't she *doing* something about it?

"And give my family the satisfaction?" the waitress said. "I'd have to hear everyone, even to third cousins, say, 'I told you so.' " She stood up. "So now I have to watch my sister drive up in her Mercedes, and I have to pretend I'm the happiest person on earth and that I don't hate every minute of my life."

Holly didn't want to hear that anyone anywhere was miserable. She didn't know what to say. After all, all she'd done was look at a handsome man with muscles bulging out of his T-shirt.

The waitress hovered over the table. "You're a nice girl so I don't want to see you get mixed up with a guy who's friends with Leon Basham."

"I won't," Holly said, but the woman kept standing there, as though waiting for Holly to say more, so she lied. "Besides, I'm engaged to be married. As soon as the movers leave, I'm going to him." When the woman still didn't leave, Holly said, "He's from an old family. His ancestors signed the Declaration of Independence."

"Any money?"

"Loads," Holly said, swallowing the lie.

The woman nodded seriously. "Just stay away from that side of the lake and those old houses. Revolution or not, what's in those houses is dangerous to girls like you."

"Revolution?" Holly asked quickly. "What revolution?"

"Nothing," the woman snapped, looking at Holly's wide eyes.

As her husband came by, he said over his shoulder, "Those old houses on this side of the lake were probably built before the American Revolutionary War. The North Carolina preservation people are trying to get them moved off the land because they're scheduled for demolition. Gonna build more of those pink houses in there." He said the last with a contemptuous look at his wife.

"Pre-Revolution?" Holly whispered, her mind whirling. "How can that be?"

"Deserters from the war," the woman said, shrugging. "Maybe English, maybe American, nobody knows for sure. The land was sold to a developer over a year ago, but somebody from the preservation society came out here and said the houses couldn't be destroyed. There was a lot about it in the local paper, and it's an on-going war."

"Who's winning?"

"It's a standoff. Believe it or not, Leon Basham is the big holdout."

"Let me guess: Because of his barn."

"You catch on fast."

Holly smiled, pushed away her half-eaten sandwich, and looked at her watch. "Look at the time! I have to go. It was delicious."

The waitress gave her a check, then went to the register to take care of some customers. Holly left a ten-dollar tip to cover the wager and maybe because the woman had tried to help Holly.

As she left the store, she remembered that she hadn't purchased anything for dinner. She decided instead she'd drive the twenty miles to a big grocery, somewhere where no one would comment if she looked at a handsome bag boy, and buy a bottle of wine, a bag of shrimp, and some corn on the cob.

But it was as though her car had a mind of its own. She turned right instead of left, and found herself heading toward the side of the lake opposite from the house her parents had rented. She'd heard her parents' guests comments on their view of the old houses. Some had been favorable, some not. Most of them agreed that their view was better than that of the people in the old houses. Her parents looked at a heavily forested hillside, the houses hidden in the trees and barely visible. But people on the other side looked at a bulldozed hill covered cheek to jowl with poorly built, monster-size houses painted in absurd colors.

Slowly, Holly drove her little Mini Cooper down the rutted road and studied the old houses that were tucked back under the trees. Most of them were difficult to see because mobile homes had been set in front of them, or they'd been covered with siding, or they were buried under voracious vines.

She drove to the end of the road, until she came to a big sign that said LAKESHORE ESTATES RESIDENTS ONLY and turned around.

It was, of course, impossible that a group of pre–Revolutionary War houses existed in western North Carolina. There were no European settlers in the area at that time. Or were there? She'd have to check her history on that.

So why were the locals saying these houses were that old?

Legend? Stories passed from one generation to another? If so, there was probably a basis in fact.

Or perhaps some preservationist had started the rumor in an attempt to save the houses. Under similar circumstances Holly would have had no qualms about that. To save an old house from destruction, yes, she'd lie.

"Lie, cheat, and steal," she said aloud and thought of Leon Basham and what he'd done for his truck. Maybe loving a truck so much was misplaced, but Holly understood. She liked passion; admired it. Lorrie had passionately loved his old house, just as his mother had. And this man Leon was in prison because he'd stolen for love of his truck.

Wonder if he stole Hollander tools? she thought as she parked her car under a drooping black walnut tree. She'd purposefully chosen a small car so she could get into tight places, and she'd ordered it in dark green so she could hide it more easily. "And it's fast so you can outrun property owners with shotguns," her stepsister had said.

Yes, it was true that Holly had an unfortunate habit of trespassing on private property to snoop through old houses. She liked to drive down curvy country lanes and see what was hidden in the woods.

Even if her methods were illegal, she'd been successful. She'd discovered a house built in 1784, that had been buried under a cheap new façade of leaky vinyl siding. She'd bought the house from the owners and had it moved to a new location. One time she'd waded through waist-high grass to find three acres covered with rotting outbuildings from an old plantation. Holly had paid to have them moved and restored. It was easy to find young couples eager to restore and live in old houses. All they needed was the money for the materials– which Holly provided.

Now, she got out of the car, looked around, and listened. When she was satisfied that no one was near, she opened the back of her car and removed the tall, triple-layered leather boots she always carried with her. Snakes loved old houses nearly as much as she did. She got her digital camera, a bottle of water, her walking stick, and a flashlight, then set off up the hill toward a house that could barely be seen under the encroaching weeds.

As soon as she got close enough, she saw that the exterior of the house wasn't very old: 1880 at the earliest. Cautiously, she stepped onto the porch, testing each board before putting her weight on it. The door had fallen off one hinge, which made it difficult to open. When she turned on her flashlight to examine the door's molding and hinges, she saw it was a replacement from the 1950s, so she gave it a shove. Some of her colleagues believed in preserving everything before 1980, but Holly wasn't one of them.

Inside, the house was in bad shape. Grapevines had taken over one side, growing through two windows like great, hairy snakes. Several floorboards had rotted through, and she could see the pale weeds growing below, inching up toward the sunlight.

She looked around the interior of the ruin, and decided she was wasting her time. Either this wasn't one of the houses considered pre-Revolutionary, or the whole idea was a hoax. She turned to leave, but then in the back she saw a beam—a large beam, maybe from a ship. Old houses were often made from dismantled ships. But here, so far inland? Cautiously, Holly made her way toward the back of the house, stepping gingerly on the floorboards, as she kept her light fastened on the overhead beam.

It was when she reached the room, saw that the beam was nothing special, that she heard the sound. The unmistakable sound of a rattlesnake. Instantly, she froze into position, her heart pounding in her throat. When she'd calmed herself enough, she turned just her head slowly in the direction of the sound. Not two feet from her was an enormous rattle-snake coiled and ready to strike if she moved even an inch. Holly had been so busy looking up at the beam that she'd almost stepped on the snake.

Stupid, stupid, stupid, she thought. Okay, so now what did she do? Wait until sundown and the cool temperature made the snake seek warmth? How about testing her snake boots? They were three layers of leather, hot beyond belief, but guar-anteed to withstand any snake bite. Guaranteed, huh? Did that mean she got her money back if they didn't work?

She told herself to stop being sarcastic and to think of a way to get herself out of there alive. No sudden movements, of course, but how about a slow, steady tiptoe out?

"Nice snake," she whispered, then swallowed when the tail rattled enthusiastically. Slowly, she stepped backward.

One second she was standing on the floor of an old house and the next she was falling through the air. She screamed in fear and shock, then let out an *oomph* as she hit bottom.

Blinking, she lay on her back and looked up. She seemed to have fallen into an old cistern. About twelve feet above, she saw the floor with its broken boards, and as she watched, the snake slithered over to peer down at her.

"That's all I need," she muttered. "Caught in a pit with a rattlesnake." Wincing with pain, bruised from the fall, she removed her camera from its case around her neck, then shot four quick photos of the snake. Blinded by the flash, it moved away from the edge.

Holly put her hand to her back and rolled a bit to one side to look around her. She was in a pit about twelve feet deep and eight feet in diameter. It had most likely once been a root cellar or used for ice storage and had probably originally had dirt or stone walls. But some industrious owner had smeared a layer of concrete over the sides, which made them slick and unclimbable.

A feeling of panic rose in Holly, but she tamped it down. Of course she could get out. Slowly, feeling her body for any injuries, she got up off the debris-covered floor. If the walls were modern enough to be concrete, then there was probably an aluminum ladder nearby.

On the floor was a foot-deep cushion of rotten wood and plants—and animal carcasses. It looked as though anything that had ever fallen into the pit had not been able to find a way out.

As she looked up at the high walls, she told herself that she was smarter than the animals, and that of course there was a way out.

An hour later, she was beginning to panic. She'd piled all the debris up and tried to climb on it, but it was so rotten her feet went through to the bottom. The decaying wood had cushioned her fall, so she hadn't been hurt, but she couldn't climb it.

Above her head were the old floorboards. She could see a rusty hinge that had once been the trapdoor that led down to the cellar. If she could latch onto the boards, could she pull herself up? Latch on with what? she wondered.

Stepping back, she took inventory of what she had to use. She had her camera in a case with a thin nylon strap. She had a bottle of water and what she was wearing. Her walking stick and flashlight had flown out of her hands when she'd fallen.

"A rope," she said as she started unbuttoning her shirt. "I have to make a rope."

# Chapter Two

HOLLY JERKED TO ATTENTION WHEN SHE HEARD the sounds above her head. Curled into a ball, wearing only her panties, her tall snake boots, and her watch, she was buried between layers of debris, trying to stay warm. Her throat was raw from screaming for help; her eyes were raw from crying in fear and frustration.

It was mine-shaft dark in the pit, her camera battery having long ago given out, and it was freezing. Although she couldn't see it, she knew that hanging above her head, dangling just above her reach, was the rope she'd fashioned out of her clothes. After two hours of work, she'd managed to catch the arm strap of her bra on a nail (modern, not square cut) protruding from a plank that had fallen to the side above the pit. She'd not tried to catch one of the rotten floor boards for fear it would break under her weight.

It had taken hours, but she'd finally managed to catch the strap on the nail.

She'd been more than halfway up when the rope broke. A seam on her shirt had given way and Holly had fallen to the bottom again. What was left of the rope dangled a foot above her outstretched hands. She'd jumped, she'd cursed, she'd leaped, but to no avail.

Darkness came quickly in the mountains and with it the cold air. Holly was alone in the forest, trapped in a concrete-lined pit, and, for the most part, naked. If she managed to live through the night, how long could she survive? If it rained she'd have drinking water, but the pit would be even colder if there was water in it.

As the sun set and the light faded, Holly did what she could to make a den out of the debris on the floor. She needed something under and over her to protect her from the cold.

What she refused to allow herself to think about was the fact that no one knew where she was. Her car was so completely hidden under trees that it might be weeks before anyone saw it. And if they did see the car, so what? This was a tourist area and there were strange cars parked everywhere.

She wouldn't let herself think that it would be weeks before her parents began to grow concerned about her disappearance. "Why do I have to be so independent!" she said, her arms clasped around her bare chest. Unfortunatley, it wasn't at all unusual for her to change her itinerary at the last moment and not show up where she'd said she'd be.

"Old houses," she said, pulling dead vines over her, then wincing because the vines had thorns in them. Her love of old houses was her downfall.

She pushed the little light button on her watch and saw that it was only ten o'clock. She would have guessed it was about 3:00 A.M. She had many hours to go before she would feel the warmth of sunlight.

When she first heard the noise above her, she opened her eyes and all her senses came alert. She'd been hearing the quiet sounds of animals moving about, but this was different. This sound came from something larger.

"Hello?" came a man's voice. "Anyone here?"

Holly was so dazed by cold, hunger, and fear that at first she couldn't respond. When she tried to speak, her throat closed entirely.

When she heard the footsteps begin to retreat, she panicked and began to kick the wall. She grabbed a rotten board and threw it upward.

"Here!" she managed to croak out. "In here!"

She held her breath when the footsteps above halted, then turned. In the next second, a flashlight was beaming down at her.

Instinctively, Holly crossed her arms over her bare chest.

"Are you all right?" A man's voice came down to her. She couldn't see his face behind the light.

"Yes," she said. "Just cold."

"Hang on a minute," he said and Holly heard a rustling noise. Seconds later, a shirt, still warm from his body, hit her face. She pulled it to her, kept it over her face for a second, then quickly put her arms in the warm sleeves.

"Thank you," she said, looking up at the light.

"Now listen to me," he said in a calm, soothing voice. "I'm going to have to take the light away for a few minutes while I look for something to use to get you out. Will you be okay?"

"You won't leave me, will you?" Holly heard the pleading tone in her voice, heard the fear.

"Leave a beautiful, naked girl alone in a pit? You think I'm crazy?"

Holly wouldn't have thought she could smile, but she couldn't help herself. When he took the light away she wrapped her arms, now clad in his long-sleeved shirt, around herself and waited. "The floorboards are rotten," she called up to him.

"I thought they might be," he said, letting her know that he wasn't too far away.

She could see the beam of his flashlight roaming about the old house. It stopped when he saw her homemade rope hanging from a fallen plank.

"I tried to make a rope," she said unnecessarily. She wanted the reassurance of his voice.

"Is that what happened? And here I thought you'd been moonbathing."

Holly relaxed more and smiled more. She couldn't see the man's face, but at the moment she'd never loved anyone as much as she loved this man—the man who'd come to save her.

"How did you find me?"

"Some woman sent the police after me."

That made no sense whatever. "Who sent the police after you? Why?" Now and then his light fell inside the pit and it always seemed to land on some animal skeleton.

"Seems you missed an appointment with the moving company."

Holly had forgotten all about them. "Yes!" she said. "I did. Did the moving company report me missing?"

"No, they reported themselves to be angry. They stopped at that store at the south end of the lake and told the couple who own it that the spoiled daughter of some government bigshot had stood them up."

Holly grimaced. With her father being an ambassador, she was nearly always assumed to be spoiled and disdainful of the "little people." She heard him moving things. "What does that have to do with you? And might I ask who you are?"

"Nick Taggert," he said, "but we haven't met. At least I haven't met you. Still okay?"

"Yes," she said, "but don't stop talking. How did the police get involved in this? Did someone see my car?"

"No." He was pulling on something and she was afraid the floor would give way and he'd end up trapped in the pit with her. But then she could climb on his shoulders and get out– unless he broke a leg in the fall, that is.

She tried to clear her head. He was talking.

"The moving men stopped at the store to get something to drink and told the woman you hadn't shown up for the appointment. She then called the police and reported a possible kidnapping, and she said that she knew who the kidnapper was."

"You?" Oh no, Holly thought. Was she being rescued by a criminal? What was he planning to do to her once he got her out of the pit? It wasn't possible that he'd put the concrete in the pit to use it as a trap to catch naked women, could it?

Holly put her hands over her face for a moment and told herself to get a grip.

"Yeah, me," he said. "The police banged on my door and demanded that I tell them what I'd done with you."

"Why would anyone think *you* had kidnapped me?"

"Try this," the man said as she heard something hit the side of the pit. When he moved his light downward, she saw a thick grapevine. "I want you to cover your hands with the shirt cuffs and hold on to the vine while I pull you up. Your knees are going to get scraped but– Wait a minute."

Holly listened to a rustling sound, then something soft landed at her feet. It was his jeans. "Put them on. They'll protect your body while I pull you up."

Holly tried to pull the jeans on over her boots but they wouldn't go, so she unlaced her boots. "Can you catch them?"

"Try me," he said, and he caught her boots easily.

Holly put on the jeans, rolled up the cuffs, and grabbed the vine.

"Don't let go," he said. "Wrap your legs and arms around the vine and cover any exposed skin so it won't be scraped."

"Okay," Holly whispered, then wrapped her body around the vine and held on while he pulled. As she went up, she thought, Whoever he is, he's certainly strong.

When she reached the top, his hands were there to steady her, and it was natural in the relief of the moment that she threw her arms around his neck. For a moment she cried, and he held her and stroked her hair. "Sssh, hush now. You're safe."

After a while, he gently pushed her away. "Let's get out of here, shall we?"

When Holly stepped back from him, they heard a thud, followed quickly by another one. When he shined his flashlight into the pit, she saw that her boots had fallen down into it.

She looked up in the darkness at the man. She couldn't see

his face or he hers, but they both knew she was asking him a question. How could she walk out barefoot?

"Okay," he said. "You wear the shirt, give me back my pants, and I'll piggyback you out of here. Sound like a good plan?"

"Perfect," she said as she held on to his arm to steady herself to remove his trousers. It was unnecessary on his part and maybe she should have protested, but he kept the light full on her, and even after she stepped out of the trousers, he kept the light on her legs. Holly was very glad she'd spent so much time working out lately.

Besides, it was odd, but she wasn't sure she'd ever felt so close to a man as she did to this one now. Except for Lorrie, that is. But then, Lorrie was the exception to every situation.

He put on his trousers nearly one-handed as he kept the light on her. Minutes later, he said, "Ready?" and she knew he'd turned his back to her.

Never in her life had she experienced anything as erotic as that walk out. The man was lean, trim, and well-muscled. He was naked from the waist up and her legs were bare. She slipped her legs around his waist, clasped her ankles, then put her arms around his bare back, her cheek on his warm skin.

"My hero," she said, trying to make a joke, but she was being too honest to make him laugh.

"Any time," he said, and clasped her ankles with one hand, the flashlight in the other.

Holly, at last released from the fear of dying in that pit, felt the warmth of his body, and as he walked through the forest, she felt herself relaxing.

"Don't go to sleep," he said. "You fell onto a concrete floor. If you're concussed you need to stay awake."

"You sound like a doctor," she murmured and wanted to kiss his warm skin.

"Basic lifesaving," he said. "Don't go to sleep."

"Mmmm," she answered, snuggling closer to him, then she awoke quickly. "Ow! Why did you do that?" He'd pinched her calf hard.

"Don't go to sleep!"

"I just want to take a bath, a long, hot bath, and—"

"Fall asleep in the tub and drown. I didn't save you to lose you. You're going home with me and I'm going to watch you all night."

"Mmmm," she said dreamily.

He'd stopped walking and she felt his movement as he opened a car door. Her car. "That tone is what started all this in the first place."

Turning, he dropped her into the passenger seat, then quickly went to the other side of the car.

What in the world was he talking about? she wondered. The driver's door opened, the dome light came on, and he slid into the driver's seat.

Wide-eyed, Holly saw that her rescuer was the man she'd

seen at the diner, the gorgeous man who'd ridden the motor-cycle. The man who was the friend of the truck lover. The man she'd nicknamed "Heaven."

He closed the door, the light went out, but he didn't start the car. "The woman at the store said you'd been 'lusting' after me and that she'd seen your car turn toward my side of the lake. When you didn't show up for the movers, she called the police and told them I'd probably kidnapped you."

"I'm sorry," Holly whispered. It was as dark in the car as it had been in the pit. Reaching out, she took his hand. She was very aware—vibrantly aware—of the fact that her bottom half and his top half were naked. So little clothing; so much skin. She remembered the cold of the pit and she hungered for warmth. "I was just watching you, and she thought . . ." Holly trailed off, not sure of what to say to explain. She took his hand in both of hers. "What made you look for me?"

"Logic," he said. "If you weren't where you were supposed to be, and you turned down this side of the lake, then maybe you were in trouble."

"I was in there for hours," she said. She hadn't meant it as a criticism that he'd taken so long, but it sounded like that. "I didn't mean—"

"That's okay. It took me a while to get over the injustice of the accusation before logic could enter my head."

" 'Injustice of the accusation,' " she said, smiling. "What does that mean? That women are never kidnapped by men? Especially by motorcycle-riding men who have a secret barn?"

"A secret–?" he began. She couldn't see his face, but she felt him turn toward her. "You're a snoop, aren't you?"

"No. That woman was afraid I'd marry you and end up working in a grocery by a lake and being jealous of my Mercedes-driving sister, so she told me about you."

He laughed, and as he did, he reached out to touch her face. Maybe he was going to feel her head to see if there were any bumps, but Holly felt too close to him for that. She moved toward him, and when his hand accidently touched her breast, a fire went through her. It was a fire ignited by life, by the joy of still being alive.

He pulled her into his arms just as she reached out to him, the console gear shift between them.

"I was so afraid," she said, her mouth on his shoulder.

"So was I. I saw your car hidden under the trees and I knew something was wrong. And I didn't know if I could get you out of that pit or not."

"But you did," she whispered, her lips close to his. "You saved me."

"Does that mean I now own you?" he whispered, teasing, as he kissed her cheek.

"I think maybe so," she said and moved her mouth so he could kiss her. She opened her mouth under his and when his tongue touched hers, she groaned.

Within seconds, their relief turned to desire, and what few

clothes they had on came off. When Nick's knee hit the gear shift, they tumbled through the opening between the bucket seats into the Mini's cavernous back.

Legs, arms, torsos entwined; lips and tongues kissed, sucked, licked. Naked, Nick went to his back and pulled Holly down on top of him. She cried out, then used her pent-up energy and her feeling that this man had given her back her life to raise and lower herself on him into a crescendo of ecstasy.

Nick lay still, his hands on her hips, lifting her, helping her, until he could stand no more, then he bent his long legs and rolled her onto her back on the seat and thrust hard into her, once, twice, four times, before collapsing on her, sweaty, sated, fulfilled.

Beneath him, Holly smiled and closed her eyes. She felt wonderful, truly wonderful.

# Chapter Three

"So now what happens?" Nick said after a few moments, and Holly knew what he meant. Did she want him to drop her somewhere? Leave it to other people to watch her all night so she didn't fall asleep? But he'd said *he* was going to take care of her. She didn't answer. Instead, she let her body go limp against the seat, one arm falling toward the floor.

"Miss Latham?" he asked, moving back from her, trying to see her face in the dark. "Miss Latham?"

Holly still didn't answer, just pretended to be asleep.

Nick sat up. "I wonder how much her father would pay in ransom?" he said softly.

When Holly's eyes flew open, he snapped on the flashlight and they smiled at each other.

"Does this mean you want to go home with me? Have me, the motorcycle man, make sure you don't sleep?"

Holly could feel her face turning red. She'd always been pretty enough that she'd never had to go after any male. They pursued her. Any man she'd ever been interested in had done *all* the chasing.

She couldn't see his face, and in spite of what they'd just done, she didn't know him very well. "I . . ." she began, then smiled. "The real truth is that I want to see what's inside your barn."

He laughed at that and Holly saw his eyes crinkle. His laugh was deep and rich and made her feel safe.

"Okay, barn it is," he said, then opened the car door to get out. When the dome light came on, Holly pulled his shirt over her and watched him. His legs were so long she wondered how he'd been able to climb through the space between the front seats. He turned away from her while he pulled on his trousers so she had a good look at the back of him, at the muscles playing under his skin, tapering down to a lean waist. His rear end was beautiful: hard and firm—and his legs were well-muscled. Did he get them from hauling engines in and out of trucks? she wondered.

Smiling, still happy she was alive, she didn't want to think about what she was doing, what she had done. She wasn't a modern woman when it came to sex. More than one girlfriend had told her that she was a throwback to the Middle Ages. Holly was the kind of girl who didn't allow a man to kiss her until the third date. Sex was months away. She'd listened to reminiscences of one-night stands, but they weren't for her.

She'd never said so, but she thought her attitude came from having "fallen in love"—as she saw it—with Lorrie when she was so young. She'd loved him and there'd been no sex. Maybe she was still searching for that ideal. Maybe, in her mind, sex and love didn't go together.

While Nick dressed, she pulled on her panties (she found them under the front seat) and slipped into the front passenger seat. When he got in the car and started the engine, she looked out at the road.

"I go home tomorrow," she said softly. "My parents are expecting me." She didn't want to elaborate even in her own mind about what she was trying to say. Was she telling him that he was good enough to rescue her, good enough to have sex with, but not good enough to, say, be seen in public with?

But he seemed to understand completely. "Then we'd better make the most of tonight, hadn't we?"

"Yes," she said, closing her eyes for a moment and thinking she was a fool. She didn't want to hurt him.

"Someone waiting for you?" he asked.

"Yes. Maybe. I think so. I haven't—" She stopped because he'd pulled the car to the side of the road, turned on the dome light, and looked at her.

"Look, Miss Latham," he said and held up his hand to stop her from saying anything. "If it's all right with you, I'd as soon not be told your first name. If you're worried that I'm going to fall in love with a society girl like you because of one night spent together, then I'll pine for you for the rest of my life, think again. I broke up with a woman weeks ago and I've been celibate since then. What I need is a lot of sex with no possibility of the words 'relationship,' 'commitment,' and especially not 'marriage.'

"My concern in all this is that if you spend twenty-four hours with me I'll spoil you forever for your little blue-blood boyfriends who'd rather play tennis than make love."

Holly blinked at him for a moment. "You'll fall in love with me," she whispered, exaggerating. "All men do."

"Twenty-four hours from now I'll pour you, exhausted, into your bed in your ugly new house and *you* will be the one who won't be able to stop thinking of *me*."

"Now why don't I believe that?" she said, smiling.

"I accept the challenge," she said, and held out her hand to shake his.

Picking up her hand, he turned it over, then looked up at her with blazing hot eyes. The next second, Holly fell onto him, the gear shift hitting her in the hip. His hands were under her shirt, running up her body onto her breasts, caressing, kneading.

The ringing of her cell phone brought her back to reality. Reluctantly, her heart pounding wildly, she pulled away from him and dug under the seat to find her big handbag and search for the phone. Her stepmother was calling, in tears of worry about her. One glance at Nick and she knew that the voices on the phone were loud enough that he could hear everything.

Nick started the car again and began driving as Holly talked to both her parents. That her stepmother was so upset was touching and her concern brought tears to Holly's eyes— and apologies to her lips. Yes, yes, she'd been trespassing yet again. Yes, she'd been snooping through some rotten old house. With a glance at Nick, she told her parents she'd been so absorbed in looking she'd forgotten about the movers.

Her father, ever the practical man, took the phone and quietly bawled his daughter out. "Yes, sir," Holly said meekly. "I'm sorry, sir." When he'd finished, he put Holly's stepsister, Taylor, on the phone.

"So what *really* happened?" Taylor asked.

As usual, Taylor was too close to whatever secrets Holly tried to keep. "So how are the wedding plans coming?" she asked, trying to distract her stepsister.

"I'll tell you everything when you get here. Wait until you see the dress I chose for you to wear. Oh," Taylor said, "Dad says to tell you that the movers will be there day after tomorrow at eight A.M. He says you're to be there, and, by the way, he wants to know why the woman at the diner thought you'd run off with some guy on a motorcycle. Did you know that Dad knows the woman's family?"

"I wouldn't doubt it. I guess Dad straightened everything out with the police."

"Of course he did. But he was giving you until midnight. If you hadn't been reached by then he was sending out the posse."

Holly glanced at Nick's profile by the dashboard light. If he hadn't rescued her, her father would have sent people to find her. She wouldn't have died in the pit after all.

When Nick glanced at her and winked, Holly smiled warmly. All in all, she was glad things had worked out the way they did. She turned her attention back to the phone. "I'll see you in two days. Don't pick out your dress until I get there."

"Pick out my dress? Aren't you quaint? You think I'm going to some bargain basement and trying them on? Daddy's flying a designer in from New York."

"Okay, so let me see the sketches. I have to go. I have something I must do. 'Bye, Taylor, and love to everyone."

Nick had pulled into the driveway in front of a dilapidated old house. "It ain't much, but it's home," he said.

She was staring at the house in the headlights, as always, trying to date the structure. Early nineteenth century, nothing in the least remarkable about it.

Nick got out and opened the car door for her. When she looked into his eyes, she forgot all about dating a house. She had twenty-four hours with this man.

"That look won't get you inside and fed," he said.

"There are different kinds of food," she answered, trying to sound sexy. But the next minute he had her bent over the hood of her car, her panties down around her ankles, and they were making love against the cold metal.

"Yes! Yes!" Holly heard herself crying out as he slammed into her.

IIis mouth covered hers to quiet her, and when he came, she was with him.

When he moved off of her, Holly had to hold on to him to steady her weak legs. Nick swept her into his arms, carried her up the stairs and onto the porch. He hesitated at the door. "The inside isn't what you're used to."

"You can't shock me. I go all over the U.S. looking inside old houses. One time I–" She broke off when Nick carried her into the house, stood her on the floor, then flipped the light switch.

It took her a moment to recover as she looked about the filthy house with its beer can tables and loose-stuffing chairs. "You don't live here," she said.

"That opinion is based on . . . ?" He raised an eyebrow in question.

"What I know of houses. This place doesn't feel lived in." She looked at him. "So where *do* you live?"

Smiling, he took a key off a hook on the wall, put his fingertips to his lips for secrecy, then led her back out the door.

He didn't have to tell her he was leading her to the barn.

Eighteen seventy, earliest, she thought when she saw the barn. There were discreet lights placed here and there that came on as they approached. Holly's trained eye saw that the dilapidated look of the barn wasn't real. It was a solid structure, and someone had spent a lot of money reinforcing the building.

She wasn't surprised to see steel doors inside the barn doors, and she almost wasn't surprised when she saw the shop inside. The name Hollander was everywhere.

Her mother had been an only child, the sole heir of Hollander Tools, but the company was run by a board of directors set up by Holly's grandfather. He'd started making precision tools out of a need and a love for them. He wasn't about to die and leave his beloved company in the hands of a daughter who wasn't interested, so he'd made sure that his daughter and granddaughter were well cared for financially, but he'd left them no control of the company itself.

Today, the only association Holly had with the company was to once a year attend a board meeting and be told that everything was going wonderfully well. The only time she'd ever used her connection to Hollander Tools was when she was thirteen. She'd called the president and asked him to please send her a full line of woodworking tools so she and Lorrie could work on his house. What had arrived had filled the old kitchen, the dairy, and the spring house.

Now, Holly looked at the truck—or maybe it should be, The Truck, since it was at the center of the magnificent workshop. Inside the cab was room for two people—slim people. Pipes ran through the glassless back window and out the side windows. The bed was full of machines and extra tires.

"So where do I put my nail file?" Holly asked, blinking up at him, and he laughed.

Companionably, he put his arm around her shoulders. "How about some food, a long bath, then some oral sex?"

"Sounds good to me," Holly said, smiling, walking with him toward one of the glassed-in rooms where she could see a kitchen. The workshop was as clean as the house was dirty.

Minutes later, he set her to chopping vegetables while he broke eggs, put toast on to grill, and squeezed fresh orange juice. He made an enormous omelet and a foot-high stack of toast. They sat side by side at the bar, legs touching from knee to hip, and shared the food, eating from one platter, sometimes feeding each other.

"So how do you know Leon?" she asked. "Is he—?" Nick put a cheese-filled bit of omelet in her mouth to silence her.

When she'd swallowed, she said, "Do you stay here often? What did those guys on the motorcycles want? Did you—?"

Again, he stuffed her mouth full.

"Okay," she said, swallowing, "I can take a hint. You could tell me—" He kissed her this time.

"I am what you see," he said.

She narrowed her eyes at him. "Girlfriend kick you out because she was starving for communication?"

He smiled, eyes twinkling. "Something like that. You want that piece of toast?"

She held the last piece of toast behind her back. "There's a price. Tell me one thing about you few, if any, people know."

"Okay," he said. "I'm a great listener. Tell me anything about yourself and I'll listen."

"That's not the kind of information I wanted."

He put his hand out for the toast and she gave it to him. "So what were you doing in that pit?"

Holly wanted to play the same game of secrecy as him, but she couldn't. She'd probably never see this man after tomorrow, so maybe she could talk to him a bit. But about what?

When she said nothing, he took her by the hand and led her to the bathroom. There was no tub, but there was a big shower and he turned on the water. In the next moment he began to unbutton his shirt that she was still wearing.

Holly took a step back. She knew it was an odd concept after all they'd done together, but showering together seemed too intimate, too personal, to do with a stranger. "Maybe this isn't such a good idea. We don't really know each other and–"

He leaned back against the countertop and Holly could see his beautiful back in the mirror. "Don't know each other? Let's see, I know that your family cares very much about you, but that you're almost afraid of your father. I know your sister is a snob and that you're terrified of being thought to be the same. I know that right now you're torn in half because you're extremely attracted to me, but you don't know how to tell me that I'm not the kind of guy you could introduce to your family. How am I doing so far?"

"Too good," Holly said with a grimace. "How'd you know all this?"

"I told you, I listen. The one thing I haven't put together is about this man in your life, the one the woman in the diner was going on about. Why wasn't he on the phone to you? Isn't he worried about you?"

It was her turn to stop him from talking. She flung her body onto his and put her face into this throat. "You're right. No talkee, just–"

He kissed her, cutting off her sentence, then he grabbed her shirt and pulled downward sharply. Buttons went flying across the tile, and in the next minute they were naked and inside the shower. Holly wanted to continue kissing, wanted to make love on the shower floor. Who would have thought that old-fashioned being-listened-to could be an aphrodisiac? Even though he'd said that all he wanted from her was sex, he'd cared enough about her to listen, to remember, and to think.

He was kissing her left ear and down her neck. "So tell me, Miss Latham, what was inside that pit with you?"

"Snakes," she said, running her soapy hands between her legs, "long, hard, slippery snakes."

"Could have fooled me," he whispered. "I would have sworn it was a family of"—he sucked on her earlobe—"skunks."

Laughing, Holly rubbed her hips against his. "So how about that oral sex?"

"Not until I clean you up," he said, his soapy hands sliding inside her.

She leaned back against the shower wall, her eyes closed, and gave herself over to the pleasure of his hands. He slid his soap-covered hands over her body, caressing her. At one point he lifted her foot, balancing it on his knee, and ran his fingers between her toes.

Never had Holly felt such sensual pleasure and she couldn't help but wonder if such pleasure was a product of his class. She'd never say to anyone, or even think out loud, that there were classes in the free American society, but there were. In her expensive boarding schools, there had always been the knowledge of what class a person belonged in. For all that Holly's mother had been an heiress, it was her father, with his illustrious ancestors, who'd put her high on the list of people to know.

The waitress at the diner thought she'd been telling Holly something she didn't know, but Holly knew firsthand how marriages to . . . to people like Nick worked out. Her stepmother had eloped with a beautiful man who owned a car repair shop. Minutes later she was pregnant, and her rich, blue-blood family had disowned her. Four years later, her husband had been killed in a car accident, and Marguerite had been left with a young daughter to support. She'd been waitressing when she'd met James Latham.

Now, as Nick's hand caressed her, she understood how a woman could run away with a beautiful man on a motorcycle. Until now, she'd been contemptuous. Self-righteous even. A girl at one of her schools had been caught having an affair with the swimming instructor. Holly had been disdainful. How could the girl have been so foolish? she'd wondered. How could she have hurt her family like that? The young man had a pregnant wife!

But now, Holly began to understand. Did all of "them" have sex lives like this? All the boys she'd ever known had . . . had. . . . Well, they didn't shower together, and they didn't bend a girl over the hood of a car.

Nick put her foot down and leaned over her face. "You're thinking," he said. "If you can think that means I'm not doing a good job."

"Not really thinking, not actually," she said as he kissed her neck. His big body was pressing her against the wall.

"What are you not actually, really thinking about?"

"No wonder you people have so many children," she said, then froze in horror at what she'd just said. "I didn't mean– I–"

"I have seven brothers and sisters," he said, seemingly unoffended. "And at least a million cousins. Cousins everywhere." He was running his hands down her body. The hot water was beating down on his back, splashing onto her face. His hands went round her thighs, parting them, sliding upward, his thumbs beginning to enter her. "Three families live in one house that constantly needs repair. We grew most of our own food."

One of his thumbs slid inside her, moving in and out in a slow, sensual way. "We lived so far away from other houses that the school bus and the mailman refused to drive to us. We didn't have TV until I was nine. I spent my days outside, fishing for the family. I was the best fisherman. I—"

"No more," Holly said, putting her hand on his cheek. "I don't want to hear anymore. Let's just—" She was going to say "enjoy the moment," but what he was doing made her stop talking—and thinking.

He had sunk to his knees and buried his face between her legs. She'd given oral sex before but had never received it. At the first touch of his tongue, her eyes widened in astonishment. In the next second, she closed her eyes and opened her legs. If he hadn't been holding her upright, she would have slid to the floor.

Just when Holly was sure she could stand no more, Nick lifted her, put her legs about his waist, and set her down on his erect maleness.

She pulled him to her, digging her nails into his back, pulling him closer and closer, wanting more and more of him. Her legs tightened, her shoulders braced against the shower wall.

When Holly came, she screamed, and Nick held her to keep her from falling. For minutes, he held her tightly against him, not letting her fall.

"You okay?" he asked after a while.

"I thought I was going to die."

She could feel him smile against her neck. "First orgasm?" he asked.

"Of course not!" she said, life returning to her limbs. "I've had a million orgasms. One for each of your cousins."

She could feel his stomach muscles moving as he chuckled, and Holly was offended. "Look, Trucker Man, just because you grew up sleeping six to a bed doesn't mean you know all about life and love and sex, while we know nothing."

Still smiling, he moved away from her, soaped his hands and began to wash her, but this time it wasn't sensual, it was "business." In the same businesslike manner, she soaped her hands and began to wash him.

"Who is 'we'?" he asked.

"I just meant–" Breaking off, she looked up at him. He had the most infuriating smile on his face, a smirk of such superiority that she wanted to wipe it off. "Your betters!" she said. "You know, those of us who give up our lives to keep the world together."

"Oh?" he said, turning her around and soaping her back. "I found you in a pit in an old house, naked, cold, and hungry. Were you planning to give up your life for that old house?"

"Not me," she said. "I meant people like my father. He–" She paused a moment as he ran his hands over her breasts.

"He what?" Nick asked huskily.

She was determined to wipe the smirk off his face. "My father flies all over the world, from one crisis to another. He has no life of his own. The phone never stops ringing. He–"

"So he sent you away to boarding schools to be raised by strangers," Nick said.

"Don't you dare say anything against my father! He was– is– You know, that's very distracting." He was massaging her breasts.

"My dad played ball with us. My uncle taught me how to ride a motorcycle. We all went to church together every Sunday." He pulled back from her, his hands on her hips. "Miss Latham, I said your sister was a snob, but so are you."

At that, he turned off the water and got out of the shower, leaving Holly sputtering behind him.

She stepped out, grabbing a towel from beside the door. He was drying himself. "I am *not* a snob! I get along with everyone. I can talk to people from all walks of life. I can–"

"You think that all of us out here are hungering for *your* life? You think that every man who grew up in a house with fewer than four bathrooms is dying to marry some over-educated, lonely, uptight, suppressed girl like you? No, Miss Latham, we are *not*."

He tossed his wet towel onto the countertop and walked, naked, out of the room.

Blinking, Holly stood there, the towel draped around her, and stared at the doorway. Over-educated? Lonely? Uptight? Suppressed? That's not how she saw herself.

Wrapping the towel around her body, she left the room. He was dressed in clean jeans and a shirt, barefoot, and rummaging inside a chest of drawers.

She tried to regain her dignity, but that wasn't easy since she was wearing only a towel and her wet hair was clinging to her face. "I think you misunderstand me," she said to his back. "I don't think that you—or people who have been raised as you have—are dying to marry people like me, but I do think that . . ." She couldn't think how to phrase what she meant to say—if she even knew what she wanted to say, that is.

He pulled some clothes from a drawer and looked at her. "You think we're all dying for your money, that we'd do anything on earth to get away from the fear of next month's electric bill. You think we all dream of getting our hands on some rich girl so we can leave our nasty little working-class lives behind." He moved toward her until they were nearly nose-to-nose. "I already know enough about your life, Miss Latham, to know I wouldn't have it on a bet. You know what my family has an abundance of? Love, that's what. When my sister got married, she didn't have some designer fly down from New York. My mother made her dress, and there was love in every stitch. Can your fancy designer top that?"

"No," Holly said softly. He was right, of course. But she had always been told that people who had less money than her family did were "less fortunate." She'd heard horror stories from her stepmother about her life with her first husband. He'd been faithless and what money he did earn, he spent on liquor.

Maybe because of the stories of the people close to her, she'd been unfair, she thought. Maybe . . .

"Put those on," Nick said, thrusting clothes into her arms. "They're Leon's, but maybe they'll fit you."

Silently, Holly put the clothes on. They were blue jeans and a worn short-sleeve shirt. She had clean, but damp, underpants, no bra, no socks, no shoes.

The atmosphere between them had changed. Nick moved to the other side of the garage where she couldn't see him, but she could feel his anger. Was it all at me? she wondered. Maybe he'd been snubbed before by someone like her. Someone like me, she thought with a grimace.

She stopped buttoning the shirt and smiled. She'd gone from thinking about "people like him" to "someone like me."

"Are you ready to go?" he asked, staring at her. His eyes were dark, his jaw set. With his unshaven whiskers, he looked like a pirate. Not exactly a turnoff.

"Go?" she said, then, "Oh." He was taking her back to her parents' rented house. It was daylight and he was finished with her.

She rolled up the cuffs of the trousers and padded after him, neither of them saying a word all the way to the car. Then, to Holly's surprise, at the end of the drive he turned left, not right. He was going toward his side of the lake, not hers.

"Where are you taking me?" she asked.

He gave her a look of surprise as he reached to the backseat and handed her her sandals. "To get your boots out of the pit, and I thought that if you wanted to see the old houses around here we might ask the owners' permission. You don't *have* to trespass, do you? It's not some deep-seated need of yours, is it?"

Leaning back against the door, she looked at him hard. Had all his anger been an act? "You have a streak of unlikability in you, you know that?"

"'Unlikability.' Did you make that word up? You know how it is with us poor, uneducated rednecks. You have to talk slow. Simple words."

"Is that so? What was it you said to me that first night? You were trying to get over the 'injustice of the accusation'? Now, I ask you, is that proper redneck talk?"

He stopped the car under the tree Holly had parked under last night. "Don't fall in love with me, Latham," he said, opening the door and getting out.

"Fat chance," she said as she got out, too. "For your information, my heart is already taken."

He opened the back of the Mini and removed a thick rope. "As long as your body is available . . ." he said, giving her a lascivious wink as he started up the hill.

At that remark, Holly thought of remaining in the car. Or maybe she should strip off and swim across the lake to her parents' house. Smiling, she thought of the shock of the neighbors if she emerged naked from the water, then walked into the ambassador's house. The next second Holly imagined the tabloid headlines.

"Are you waiting for me to carry you? Again?" Nick asked from above her.

"So when do you get horny and start being nice to me again?" Holly snapped.

Seriously, Nick looked at his watch. "About thirty-two minutes. Can you wait that long?"

Holly had to work to keep from laughing, but she kept her face straight. "Make it twenty-eight minutes," she said, deadpan.

"Deal. Now get your cute little rear end up here. If I get trapped in that pit, you have to go for help."

"Yes, sir," she said, and started up the hill behind him.

"Good attitude."

"That does it. Next time *you're* on top and you do *all* the work."

"Same ol', same ol'."

She'd reached him so she smacked him on the shoulder. His arm flashed out and he pulled her to him and kissed her deeply. When he moved his mouth away, he looked into her eyes and smiled. "Stop worrying so much. Don't worry about me; don't worry about you. Seize the moment. Enjoy. Let tomorrow take care of itself. Okay?"

Nodding, she smiled back at him, and just when he looked as though he was going to kiss her again, she said, "Do you think there really are any pre–Revolutionary War houses up here?"

He released her, but he was smiling. "You're obsessed, aren't you?"

"Completely." She was following him cautiously, stepping on the weeds he'd smashed flat. Wearing sandals where she knew there were poisonous snakes didn't exactly relax her. "You should have brought a ladder," she called after him.

Nick held up the rope as though that were an answer. And it was, for he'd then proceeded to knot the rope and use it to climb into the pit to retrieve her boots. He also retrieved the rope she'd made out of her clothes so she at last had a bra to wear.

"Ready?" he said when they were finished at the house.

"For what?"

"To see your houses."

"Yes," she answered, then took the hand he held out to her and followed him down the hill to the car.

## Chapter Four

It was 8:00 p.m. and Holly was eating an enormous plate of pasta in a spicy tomato sauce that she and Nick had made together. She was very tired, hadn't been to bed since two nights ago, but she didn't know when she'd ever felt better. She and Nick had had a wonderful day!

He was new to the community, but he fit in with the people. They seemed to feel that he was one of them. He chatted easily with everyone they met, and always seemed to know what to say to whom.

For the most part, Holly had felt awkward and hadn't known what to say. "Could I please see the falling-down old house behind your mobile home?" didn't cut it. Years ago, when she was just starting out, clipboard in hand, she'd knocked on doors and asked. The reactions had been varied, but pretty much all had been negative.

But when she was with Nick, doors were thrown open in

welcome. During the entire day she didn't think he ever once asked anyone directly to be allowed to enter an old structure on their property. He'd introduced himself as being "a guest of Leon and Carl Basham" and gone from there. He chatted and made comments about their houses and their gardens, and before long he and Holly were being escorted around the place—including a trip through the old houses and barns.

At two they'd gone back to Leon's barn and made sandwiches.

"Did you see anything interesting?" Nick had asked after they'd made love. All morning he'd taken every opportunity to touch her. At the first of his unexpected, intimate caresses she'd squealed out loud and Nick had made excuses for her. Two hours later, they were standing behind a window, chatting with the owner, while Nick's hand caressed the back of her thighs. Other than the bead of sweat on her forehead, Holly had shown no change in expression.

However, by the time they broke for lunch, both of them were at a fever pitch of excitement. Once inside Leon's garage, they charged at each other, tearing clothes off each other's bodies in a frenzy, with their lips glued together all the while. They made love on the cold, hard concrete floor, Holly's head jammed against the tire of The Truck.

Afterward, they'd showered, made enormous sandwiches, and Nick asked her about what she'd seen.

"Nothing particularly old; nothing unique, which is a shame because the buildings probably won't be saved."

"No rescuing preservation society?"

"No," she said. "There's no Belle Chere here." As soon as she said the name she wished she hadn't. Perhaps Nick wouldn't notice.

"I see," Nick said, refilling her glass with lemonade. "And is he the one who's taken your heart?"

His odd question was so right on that she choked and coughed, unable to breathe for what seemed like minutes. When she could speak she said, "Of course not. Belle Chere is a place, not a person."

"Maybe to the world, but when you say the name, you caress it. You roll it around on your tongue and taste it. Is it sweet? Salty? Sour? Bitter? Or is it all of those things?"

Holly couldn't keep from smiling. Whatever else he was, he was perceptive to the point of wizardry. "All of them," she said, then filled her mouth with a bite of sandwich so she could say no more.

"You know that thing I did with my tongue this morning in the shower?" He glanced downward. "That thing you liked so much?"

Mouth full, she nodded.

"Talk or it won't happen again."

She swallowed. "Didn't the Geneva convention declare that particular torture to be unfair in war?"

"Before my time. Who and what is Belle Chere?"

Holly had to take a few breaths while she decided what to tell him. For too many years she'd not allowed herself to talk about either Lorrie or his plantation. But perhaps if she told about the place and left out the man it would be all right.

"Belle Chere has been blessed by poverty," she began, and once she started she couldn't stop. She went on to tell him how the house had been built by Lorrie's very rich English ancestors in 1735. He'd been a younger son so his older brother had inherited the family mansion in England. In an attempt to re-create the opulence of his childhood home, he'd spared no expense when he built Belle Chere in the American colonies. Every room had been paneled; every piece of plaster work had been shaped or frescoed.

For years Belle Chere had been a gentleman's estate, used for breeding racehorses, but in the 1820s the four thousand acres of parkland had been cleared for farmland. It was the heyday of slavery and Belle Chere had been made into a plantation. Outbuildings of dairy, icehouse, smokehouse, office, and slave quarters had been erected. Six acres had been planted in symmetrical box-bordered pleasure gardens and orchards.

Belle Chere had managed to escape Sherman's torch at the end of the Civil War and the owners had retreated to their house and gardens, trying to preserve what they had.

Over the years they sold off most of the land, until there were only a hundred and thirty acres left.

"They used what money they had to maintain, never to renovate," Holly said.

"What's the difference?"

"When a house is lived in for generations, people add to it and tear down parts that they don't like. They change a house constantly. They add electricity to the old kitchen, cut in a few more windows, tear out the fireplace to build a barbeque, then they decide they're sick of the old building so they run a bulldozer over it and put up some prefab monstrosity."

"But I take it that they didn't do that at Belle Chere."

"No. It was in the same family for centuries, and there was always at least one family member who truly loved it so he or she did what they could to preserve Belle Chere as it was. They kept the outbuildings from falling to the ground, and they preserved the gardens. They kept the hedges alive enough to see where the *parterres* had been. They couldn't afford to fill the beds with thousands of bulbs and the roses died, but at least they didn't plow the decorative gardens under and plant beans."

"Preservation," Nick said. "Status quo."

"Yes. Today Belle Chere is run-down and, maybe to the uninitiated, it looks bad, but it's the purest, most untouched plantation site in America."

"Ah," he said.

"What does that mean?"

"You want it. But how much do you want it?"

"How much do I want Belle Chere?" she asked, smiling. "It's not for sale. I told you that it's been owned by the same family since it was built. Can you imagine that?"

"Aren't there some houses in Virginia on the James River that are still owned by the people who built them?"

She looked at him sharply. "How do you know that?"

"I worked there for a few summers. Repairing roofs and general carpentry."

"Oh," she said. "Yes, a family named Montgomery owns those houses, but they're very rich and they maintain the houses perfectly. Belle Chere is . . ."

"A fixer-upper. Something you could get your lovely little hands on and renovate."

She smiled in answer.

"So where would you get the money?"

"From—" she said, then took a drink. She'd almost said, "From Hollander Tools," but she'd caught herself. Through the glass wall she could see into the garage. The distinctively written name of Hollander seemed to be on every surface. "Donations," she said at last. "Lots of very wealthy people donate to restore old buildings."

"Like the Montgomery family?"

"Yes. I've met some of them. Very nice people, and generous with their donations."

"So who owns Belle Chere now?"

"The Beaumonts. I believe the current owner's name is Laurence."

"Larry Beaumont," Nick said.

"Lorrie," Holly said before she thought and Nick turned to look at her.

"What?!" she said. "I've met him. So what? He's a nice man and he loves Belle Chere. He'll be the one to keep it for the next generation."

Nick drank his lemonade, his face turned away, staring straight ahead toward the interior of the garage. "What does he look like?"

"Tall, blond. Good looking, if you like that sort."

"And you're in love with him," Nick said as he got up to put his plate in the sink.

"That's ridiculous."

"Oh? How far is this Belle Chere from where you're going to meet your parents?"

Holly's face turned red.

"Come on, Latham, what are you up to? And don't try to make me believe you're not going after what you want. I saw how determined you were to get to see an old house. If you brave snakes and pits for a piece of rubbish, what would you do to get your beloved Belle Chere?"

"I wouldn't do anything. The truth is, I met Lorrie before I ever saw Belle Chere."

"And loved both at first sight," he said, and again her face turned red.

Smiling, Nick smacked her on her jean-clad fanny. "You want to go with me to see some more houses, or go back to your place and daydream about some old house and some washed-out, blond rich kid?"

"Hmm," Holly said, as though she were contemplating the question.

When Nick picked her up, twirled her around, and made her laugh, it was as though something was released inside her. Hidden away, buried for years, was her secret love for Lorrie Beaumont. Never had she been tempted to tell anyone about him. That summer she'd managed to keep her parents and her stepsister from finding out about him. In fact, at the end of the summer there'd been a dance at the local country club and her father had introduced her to Lorrie and his parents.

Maybe it was Nick's teasing or the fact that she never planned to see him again, but she soon found herself telling him about the summer when she was thirteen, the glorious summer she'd spent with Lorrie.

In fact, once she started, Holly talked so much that she didn't notice that Nick drove past the last two old houses without stopping. At the end of the road, near the sign that said NO TRESPASSING, Nick pulled Holly from the car.

"He taught me how to strip paint," she was saying, "and I can tell you that I've used that knowledge hundreds of times since then. One summer in college I was allowed to work with Dr. Abernathy because I already knew enough to be useful to him. If it hadn't been for Lorrie— Where are you going?" Dazed, she looked around her. Nick had disappeared into the trees.

Minutes later, he emerged, pulling a beat-up old wooden canoe out of the forest.

"I saw this a couple of days ago. It looks like it's in good shape so I thought we might test it out."

Holly looked at it dubiously. She'd been on yachts before and the brawny crew members had rowed them to shore, but could Nick?

He seemed to read her mind. "I can do something besides ride a motorcycle. Get in."

She was quiet for a few minutes as Nick pushed the old canoe into the water, then easily used the oars to guide them onto the lake. It was too early in the season, and too cool for the people in the Easter egg–colored houses across the lake, so they were the only people on its smooth surface.

"So when did you two get together again? As adults?"

The sun was going down, Holly hadn't had any sleep for a long time, and she was sexually satisfied in a way she'd never been before. She was dozing off.

"Latham!" Nick, said sharply, waking her. "Don't wimp out on me now. You can sleep tomorrow. When did you and your rich boyfriend get together after his summer of free child labor?"

Languidly, Holly trailed her fingers in the water. "Never. I haven't seen Lorrie since that summer. Not in person, that is. There are photos and stories about him on the Internet."

"You haven't seen him since you were thirteen years old?" Nick asked, incredulous.

Holly narrowed her eyes at him, but didn't answer.

After a while, Nick smiled. "I want the truth. How far from Belle Chere is the house your parents bought?"

"Miles," Holly said, her mouth in a rigid line.

"How long does it take you to get to his house by water?"

"You really aren't a likable person. Has anyone ever told you that before?"

Nick was rowing and chuckling. "Amazing," he said at last. "You are so obsessed with some fantasy summer you think you had that you've moved heaven and earth to get near this poor, unsuspecting guy."

At that, Holly started to stand up, but when the boat tipped, she sat back down, her arms folded across her chest. "You're despicable. I'm sure your girlfriend had good reason to break up with you."

Nick kept rowing, kept smiling. "It is fascinating to see how the mind of a woman works. Let me guess. You found out that your childhood boyfriend was going to be at home this summer so you, somehow, managed to coerce your unsuspecting parents into buying the house a few miles down the river—"

"Less than one mile," Holly said. She gave him a look of reproach, but she couldn't help smiling. He seemed to be honestly amazed at what she'd done—and not a little admiring.

"And no one suspected?"

"My stepsister knows I'm after something, but I don't think she has any idea what."

"She probably thinks you want Belle Chere."

"I do! I mean, I want the house, but I want the man, too. He really is perfect for me."

Nick was quiet for a moment. "You were thirteen. Did you two . . . ?"

"No!" Holly said emphatically. "Lorrie never touched me. He was like a big brother to me, only I . . . I . . ."

"Lusted after him. I hear you do that with men. Okay, so what's going on with him in the real world?"

"He's a lawyer and he wins big cases, so I can follow him on the Internet. He was divorced last fall and he told some society columnist that he was going to take a sabbatical this summer and stay at his family home."

"Belle Chere?"

"Oh, yes."

"I see," Nick said, shaking his head in wonderment. "It looks like we men don't have a chance once a woman decides she wants us."

"You're disgusting."

"You said that."

"Bears repeating."

"I just want to give it a chance. Is that so bad? I liked him and he liked me, but that was when we were both very young. Now we're grown-ups and we're both free so I thought maybe . . ." She looked up at him, and didn't like that she wanted his approval.

"So what am I?" Nick asked. "A sort of prebachelorette party? One last fling before you marry your blueblood and move into the old homestead?"

Holly thought of defending herself but didn't. "More or less, that's exactly what you are."

"No chance that you and I . . . ? That we could . . . ?" He wiggled his brows as though asking if they could set up housekeeping together.

Holly looked away, frowning. Unfortunately, she was beginning to like him. Sure, he made her body sing—and cry and writhe—but then other men had. . . . Actually, no man had come close to making her feel as Nick Taggert did. But another man *could!* she told herself. With love and practice, a man could make her feel . . .

When she looked up at him, the fading light glinting off his dark hair, she again thought how he looked like a pirate. He was so very good-looking. Heaven, she thought, smiling to herself. The first time she saw him she'd thought of him as "Heaven."

"No," she said, after a while. There was regret in her voice, but, as always, she was a realist. "There can be nothing between us." It was one thing to spend a sleepless weekend having fabulous sex with a man who rode a motorcycle and slept in his friend's garage, but you didn't *marry* men like him. She didn't want to end up like her stepmother had, with a man who spent his evenings at the local bar shooting pool. And she didn't want to end up with a man who was so intimidated by her inheritance that he came to hate her. She'd seen that happen, too.

"Sorry," she murmured. She tried to sound nonchalant, but she felt guilty. For a moment she had a flash of an old, fat Nick, surrounded by kids, a wife with her hair in curlers and a cigarette between her thin lips. "I used to know her," Nick would say when he saw Holly on TV on Lorrie's arm, as they attended some gala.

"Sorry for me?" Nick asked, smiling. "You spent an entire summer alone with a sixteen-year-old boy, he didn't touch you, and *you* feel sorry for *me?*"

"Just because you people–I mean . . ." she said, trailing off.

"Yes, what about 'us'? You think we think only of sex? We have nothing else in mind? We don't think of compatibility? Whether or not we have anything in common?"

"I didn't–I don't mean–" Holly began, then stopped. "Are you hungry?"

"I've been told that the store down the road doesn't sell caviar."

"Very funny." She was silent for a moment. "Nick, you're going to be okay, aren't you?" she asked quietly.

"You mean, am I going to pine for you for the rest of my life? Compare all women to you and find them wanting?"

She smiled at the way he put it.

"Maybe a little," he said, smiling back. "You are one hot cookie in bed."

She was pleased, but embarrassed at the same time, and a horrible thought came to her. "You wouldn't . . . you know, mention this to anyone, would you?"

"Tell your boyfriend about us?" he asked, still smiling. "You are a throwback, you know that? Will this guy think you're a virgin?"

"No, but my father does," Holly said and they laughed together.

After that, they'd returned to Leon's garage and made a huge pot of spaghetti, and when she was full, Holly's energy left her. She fell asleep with her head on the table. The next thing she knew, Nick was lifting her in his arms and carrying her to her car.

"Sorry," she said again, unable to open her eyes.

"I want to give you something," Nick said, but Holly could hardly hear him. Her mind was too fuzzy with sleep. "It's a necklace," he said. "Promise you'll wear it."

"Mmmm," was all she could say. She managed to open her eyes a bit and smile at him, but she was still mostly asleep.

Vaguely, she was aware that he slipped something around her neck, then started the car. The next thing she knew he was carrying her up a flight of stairs. When he put her down on a bed, Holly let herself sink into oblivion.

# Chapter Five

"GOOD-BYE, LATHAM," NICK SAID, KISSED HER FORE-
head, then left the house.

He walked back to Leon's house on the far side of the
lake, glad for the exercise because it gave him time to think.
By the time he reached the barn/garage, he was telling himself that by tomorrow he'd never remember the woman. All
that had been between them was sex and nothing else. He'd
had a great time with a funny, smart, interesting, beautiful
young woman, but now it was over. She was going to her
parents' home and probably make a fool of herself over
some snob she'd had a teenybopper crush on, but that was
her business. After seeing the way she'd lusted over the old
houses they'd seen together, Nick thought that as long as
Holly had some old plantation house, she might be happy.

So why was he feeling so rotten? Was it vanity? He'd never
been turned down by a woman before. Women thought he

looked good and they knew his family had money, so Nick had never had any problem in that department.

But now, in an unusual set of circumstances, his family's wealth and prestige were not a part of the picture and what had happened? A girl he'd really liked had told him thanks, but no thanks. She'd told him he was okay to bed, but not to wed.

When Nick got back to the barn, he went through the long ritual of unlocking it, then stood in the doorway and looked about the place. Without her there, the garage was too big, too brightly lit, and too . . . too silent. He already missed her laughter.

Yawning, he went into the office and began cleaning up the kitchen. He was tired and he knew he should go to bed, but he didn't want to. He wanted to snuggle up to . . . to her.

What had he been thinking when he'd said he didn't want to know her first name? He'd known where her wallet was so he could have looked, but he didn't.

"The hell with it!" he said, then went to Leon's fax machine. Maybe it would be easier to forget her if he knew she was going to be all right. Maybe he'd feel better if he knew that the man she was after was a good man. Maybe–

He stopped making excuses, then wrote out a fax to send to his cousin Mike. Nick asked him to send information about Ambassador James Latham's youngest daughter, and about a man named Laurence Beaumont, who owned an old plantation called Belle Chere.

Once the page went through, Nick went to bed.

The ringing of the phone woke him. Groggily, he awoke, heard the sound of a fax machine, then lay still for a while, not fully awake. For minutes, he lay there, half-asleep, and wished Latham was with him. He'd like to run his hands up her bare legs. Did she wear pajamas or a nightgown to sleep in? Maybe she slept in nothing. Or in silk. Maybe black silk. Or red. How about a deep pink that would look good against her pale skin? Maybe . . .

The beep of the fax machine brought him back to reality. Someone had sent him a fax and it had finished printing.

Nick flung back the sheet and went to the machine to retrieve what looked to be about ten pages of faxed sheets. He'd only read one of them when he had to sit down.

"Hollander 'Holly' James Latham," he read. "Hollander Tools heiress . . ." "Millions on her twenty-first birthday." There was a long list of restoration projects she was working on or had completed. According to the dates, some of them had been started when she was just seventeen.

There was a sheet entitled "William Laurence 'Lorrie' Beaumont." "Father committed suicide over land scandals . . . Massive debt . . . Married to a very rich widow ten years his senior . . . Preservationists who want Belle Chere turned down."

Nick scanned the pages and didn't like what he read. It didn't surprise him to find out that Holly—that was her name—was wealthy. He smiled when he remembered that they'd made love on top of a floor dolly with the name "Hollander" painted across it.

What Nick didn't like was what he read about the Beaumont family. Holly had said that since the house was built, there had been at least one family member who was obsessed with Belle Chere enough to keep it restored.

This Lorrie's father had committed suicide, presumably because he was so deeply in debt. Lorrie had married an heiress ten years older than he was. Maybe it was love, but maybe it was . . .

Nick put the pages down and told himself he was being ridiculous. He'd lost the girl to someone else. Lost fair and square.

Well, maybe not fair and maybe he'd not been square with Holly about who and what he was, but he couldn't bear to see her eyes change. He couldn't have taken it if she'd suddenly said she would see him again now that she knew he was a doctor and of a good family.

No, Nick couldn't bear that. He wanted a woman to love him for himself, not for his status, not for his family's money.

"So why'd you give her the diamond?" he muttered aloud. His cousin Mike'd had some sharp things to say when he found out Nick had given the big canary diamond to his girl-friend. "Wife, Nick," Mike said. Not yelling, not angry, but in a tone far worse. "Wife. There's a difference."

There'd been a horrible scene when Nick had told

Stephanie Benning she had to give the necklace back to him.

And now Nick had draped the multimillion-dollar stone around Holly's pretty little neck. "You're an idiot, Taggert," he said, then couldn't keep from smiling. It looked like he'd have to go to her house across the lake and get the necklace back. Darn.

As he was thinking about this, another fax came through. There was a cover letter from Mike.

"I don't know what you're up to, but I saw a photo of Ambassador Latham's daughter, so I can guess. However, we received an odd phone call from the police around Lake Winona. They seemed to believe you're a lowlife, semicriminal who might have tried to kidnap an innocent young lady. I didn't understand any of it until I got your request for info on Miss Hollander James Latham.

It's none of my business what you're doing, but I thought you might be interested in this help wanted ad. If the job has been filled and you want it, let me know and I'll hire him away.

> Good luck.
> With love,
> Mike

P.S. Maybe you should return the necklace to the family vaults until vows are exchanged."

Nick had a momentary feeling of guilt over the necklace, but he smiled as he took a sheet of paper and wrote "I want the job" in big letters on a piece of paper, then faxed it through to his cousin.

Nick made himself a huge breakfast, then got on the phone. First, he had to take care of his job. His cousin could take over for him. She was fresh out of medical school and what she lacked in experience she would make up for in enthusiasm.

A few more calls got his mail, utilities, and his apartment taken care of. He didn't want any of his "doctor clothes," clothes whose labels would give too much away.

By late afternoon he was ready to call the number in the ad. It was a want ad for a caretaker for a small estate in North Carolina, a jack-of-all-trades man to live in a small cottage on the grounds to look after the gardens, the boat, and the pier. It gave no indication that the employer was Ambassador James Latham, but Nick knew it was.

The phone was answered by an angry man. It seemed the first person he'd hired had just quit. "The grass is to my ankles and my daughter has chiggers. Do you know what those are?" It was the commanding voice of a man used to speaking in public—and used to having people obey him.

"Yes, sir, I do," Nick said. And I know where to scratch your daughter's itch, he wanted to say.

The "sir" seemed to mollify him. "How soon can you be here?"

"About nine hours," Nick said.

"Then do it. The lawnmower is in the shed by the garage. Your house is the white one by the water. I like employees in direct proportion to how little attention I have to pay to them. Do your job, stay out of my sight, give me no problems, and I'll frequently raise your salary. Understand me?"

"Yes, sir. I'll–" Nick said no more because Ambassador Latham had hung up on him.

For a moment Nick stared at the phone. Was he sure he wanted to do this? It wasn't as though he was in love with Miss Hollander Latham. Just because he'd spent two fabulous days with her and now he could think of nothing else in the world was no reason to subject himself to a summer of lawn mowing. And boat maintenance. And chiggers. And more fabulous sex.

Smiling, Nick looked at his watch. He could be at Spring Hill in eight hours. He'd given himself an extra hour to go to a local store and buy a wardrobe of T-shirts and jeans.

# Chapter Six

"HOLLY, DARLING," MARGUERITE LATHAM SAID from across the dining table, "you look exhausted. Aren't you sleeping well?"

Holly caught herself before her chin fell into her soup. It might be canned tomato soup, but it was served in Wedgwood china, on Irish linen, and an eighteenth-century mahogany table.

"What's wrong with you?" her father asked from around his newspaper.

"Nothing, sir," Holly said. "I was up late . . . studying." She swallowed because she wasn't good at lying.

"So who have you met?" Taylor, across from her, asked.

Holly tried to kick her stepsister under the table, but Taylor moved her long, slim legs out of the way. Growing up, Taylor had been Holly's closest friend. Together they'd been shuffled from one school to another, moved from one country to another. Taylor had been ten years old when her mother had married James Latham. She'd lived a life of poverty and deprivation, but she'd adjusted to being an ambassador's daughter in an amazingly short time. "I always knew I didn't belong in a fourth-floor walk-up," she'd told Holly when Holly was still a kid and Taylor was a gorgeous, elegant, sought-after young woman.

Because they knew each other well, Taylor knew Holly was lying, and from the look on Taylor's face, she meant to find out why Holly was nearly falling asleep at the table.

But Holly also knew Taylor. She turned to her stepmother. "Didn't you say you planned to use gardenias in the centerpieces at the wedding? I read that gardenias are so very 'last season.' "

"Last season!" Taylor exclaimed. "What idiot wrote that? Gardenias are always in fashion. They denote old-world culture, southern charm. Charles's family is nothing if they aren't southern. They epitomize—"

"How a turncoat can flourish," James said, putting down his paper. He'd had a minion do some research and found out that when the American Revolutionary War started, Charles Maitland's ancestors had been on both sides, English and American. They'd waited until they saw who won before settling on the American side. They'd stood back and watched the newly formed American government confiscate hundreds of thousands of acres from families that had remained loyal to the king, but the Maitlands kept their land. Not that they still owned their ancestral land, but they still had the name–and money made from cotton and peanuts.

"Father," Taylor said in a voice of exasperation, "that was hundreds of years ago. Before Charles was born. I think it's time to forget, even if you can't forgive. I think–"

As Holly bent her head over the soup, she could feel her stepsister's eyes bearing down on her, willing Holly to lift her head and look at her.

But Holly didn't look up because she was afraid the guilt would show in her eyes. It was, of course, absurd, but she was afraid her family would see in her eyes where she'd spent her last days.

She well knew that Taylor had indulged in more than one weekend with some man she'd never see again, but Holly hadn't. She had–

The overpowering noise of a lawnmower just outside the window made her look up.

"Damnation!" James Latham said, pushing back his chair and going to the door. "Turn that thing off!" he bellowed. There were few people on earth who could be heard above a powerful lawnmower, but the ambassador was one of them. Instantly, the noise stopped and Mr. Latham went back to his chair, then looked at his BLT sandwich with disdain. "When does the cook arrive?"

"Tomorrow, dear," Marguerite said. Perhaps because she

was waitressing when she met her second husband, she refused to make anything more than canned soup and simple sandwiches–although both girls knew she was quite an accomplished cook. Once, she'd told the girls, "If your father found out I can cook, he'd put yet another responsibility on my shoulders and I have quite enough already, thank you." She was right. James Latham believed his job was to sort out the world and his wife was to take care of everything else. Now that he was retired, he saw no reason to change.

"So, Dad," Taylor said, "who is the gorgeous hunk you hired to mow the grass?" Taylor loved to antagonize her stepfather. Whereas Holly was half-afraid of him, Taylor loved to push the man to the point of rage.

"Taylor, I don't think–" Marguerite began, always the peacemaker.

"Have you seen him?" Taylor asked Holly.

"No," Holly said sleepily. Yesterday the movers had shown up at 6:00 A.M. and, probably to get her back for standing them up, they'd had a thousand questions an hour–all on different floors. She'd spent the day running up and down stairs. But as exhausted as she was, that night she'd not been able to sleep. All she'd thought about was Nick. She thought of his arms, of his face nuzzling her neck. She thought of the way he'd run soapy hands over her body. At 3:00 A.M. she got up, got into her car, and drove to his house. There was no answer to her knock. Feeling as though he'd rejected her, she'd returned to the summer house, packed her clothes, and started the drive to her parents' house. Yet again, she'd had another night of no sleep.

"I can tell you that if I didn't have Charles, I'd–"

"Run off with the lawnmower boy?" Marguerite asked, horror in her voice. The only time she was a snob was when the life partners of her daughters came into consideration.

"Maybe I'd just spend a weekend or two–or six–with him," Taylor said, obviously trying to provoke her stepfather, but he was ignoring her.

Eating his sandwich with a knife and fork (James Latham did *not* touch food with his hands), he looked at his wife and said, "So what invitations do we have?"

"The usual. The Edenton Historical Society wants your endorsement, and there are a few teas."

"Humph! Little old ladies who think they should wear hats when they meet me. What else?"

"All the churches. One has asked you to give the sermon."

"Possible," he said. "Possible. Perhaps I– Now what?!" Outside came the noise of a weedwhacker. Tossing his napkin onto the table, he got up, went to the door, and bellowed again, "Turn that thing off!" When it was silent, he said, "Bother me with that noise again and you're fired." He paused as the new gardener seemed to be talking. "Then do it by hand!" was Ambassador Latham's answer.

"Machinery!" he said, sitting down once again. "Now, where were we? Oh yes, invitations."

"Some dinner parties."

"Any of them interesting?"

"No. Oh yes. Remember that nice young man who lived down the river? He had an unusual first name. Something from *Little Women.*"

"Jo?" Taylor asked.

With each word her stepmother spoke, Holly's sleepiness fell away. Lorrie's mother had loved the book *Little Women* and it was she who called her son "Lorrie" instead of "Larry."

"Lorrie," Holly said, trying to sound unconnected to the name.

"Yes, that's it. Didn't you two spend time together that summer when you were eleven?"

"Thirteen," Holly said, her head bent low over her plate.

"Yes, I guess so," Marguerite said. "Anyway, he's back here for the summer and he's invited us to . . ." She trailed off.

When Holly looked up, her family was staring at her and she grinned. They knew her passion for old houses and they assumed she'd remembered Lorrie's name because of his house. "Belle Chere," Holly said. "A plantation that hasn't been remodeled and is perfectly preserved. When I saw it when I was thirteen, the blacksmith's tools were still in the shop. Even the icehouse was still standing. Do you know how difficult it is to find an icehouse that hasn't collapsed? And the–"

"Yes, dear," Marguerite said loudly. "Shall I accept his invitation for dinner at Belle Chere on Saturday night?"

All Holly could do was nod. Yes, oh yes, oh yes, she wanted to shout. Smiling, she looked at her father and Taylor, saw that their eyes were glazed over in anticipation of one of Holly's speeches on the incomparable beauty of some derelict old house.

After a moment, Taylor leaned across the table and said, "So why did *you* decide to spend the summer here?"

For a moment Holly didn't know what she meant, but then the three of them laughed and she turned away in embarrassment—and triumph. They thought she'd returned for a house, not a man. Good! Beyond anything, she didn't want anyone to think that she was after a man. If it got back to Lorrie that she was after him, his pride would make him turn the other way. The only chance she had of winning Lorrie Beaumont was to get him to pursue her.

Shouldn't be too difficult, she thought. She'd managed to get the handsome Nick Taggert to want her. Of course, when she'd met him she'd been naked and inside a pit and—

She broke off her thoughts because outside the dining room window she saw the back of a man's head. He was hidden from view from the neck down, but from the back he . . . he looked like Nick.

"That's him," Taylor said in a loud whisper, as though she didn't want her stepfather to hear. "Divine, isn't he?"

"Taylor, if you must show your origins, kindly keep them from my daughter." He was referring to the fact that Taylor's biological father had been a good-looking hoodlum.

Taylor was unperturbed. She knew that what her stepfather hated most on earth was a coward. He believed a person should stand up for himself whether he was right or wrong— wrong being whatever didn't agree with James Latham. "From Hollander?" Taylor asked innocently, batting her lashes at the ambassador. Socially, her father and Holly's mother had been the same.

James Latham pushed his chair away from the table. "Accept everything," he said to his wife. "Especially the sermon. Perhaps I'll change careers and become a man of the cloth. Holly, my dear, might I suggest that you prepare an outline of your dissertation and I'll go over it with you. And, Taylor," he said with a sigh, "stay away from the lawnmower boy. He needs the job. And you," he said, looking at his wife, "you—"

"James," she said forcibly, "I can organize my own time."

"Yes, just so," he said, then picked up his newspaper and went up the stairs to his study where the three women knew that he'd take a nap.

Once the ambassador was out of the room, the three women leaned back in their chairs in relief.

"How long has he been like this?" Taylor asked.

"Since his heart attack," Marguerite answered. "He's tried

to make Phyllis, Roger, and me into his entire staff. The first gardener quit after just two days. I can't imagine why he stayed that long. After today I assume this one will leave. Do either of you know how to mow a lawn?"

"No idea," Taylor said with a shudder. "Oh no, look at the time. I have a fitting in an hour. Holly, when are you going to get fitted for your bridesmaid dress?"

"Taylor, that dress isn't really lavender chiffon, is it?"

"And what's wrong with that?"

"Unlike you, I have hips. I have breasts," Holly said. "I'll look like one of those pillow dolls from the twenties."

"And who knows what that looks like?" Taylor said.

"Anyone want some ice cream?" Marguerite asked.

Holly said no; Taylor said yes. As soon as they were alone, Taylor lowered her voice. "So why did you miss the movers?"

"I told you, I fell into a pit and I had a difficult time getting out."

"Mmmm-hmmm. Sure. So why did the police call here and ask if you'd been kidnapped?"

"A misunderstanding," Holly said, looking away. "I think maybe I'll take a nap. I'm sure there'll be some wonderful social event tonight that'll keep me out late and—"

"You look great, you know that?"

"Thanks," Holly said, smiling in appreciation of the compliment.

"No, really, you look the best I've ever seen you look."

"I lost a few pounds and toned up a bit, so–"

"No. Not that. It's something else. There's a glow around you. Who's the man?"

Holly thought she'd better stop this right now. She looked toward the kitchen, then back. "It's anticipation. I'm going to try to get this man, Lorrie Beaumont, to allow me to research Belle Chere so I can write about it. My dissertation will be the history of one house."

"And the thought of a summer spent digging through two hundred-year-old papers is making your cheeks glow and your eyes sparkle?"

"Yes, of course," Holly said, trying hard not to blink at the lie.

"Try again."

"That and two days of the most divine sex ever experienced on earth," Holly said at last, feeling the necklace Nick had given her tucked into her bra.

Taylor leaned back in her chair and smiled. "Good for you. So who was he? Anyone you can bring home to Mommy and Daddy?"

"Far, far from it," Holly said, sighing. "Think motorcycles and racing trucks and Hollander Tools."

"Are you going to give him an employee discount?"

"I'm never going to see him again. Over. Done with. I'm now going to turn my head to my studies and an appropriate man. Does Charles have a brother?"

"Charles is an only child, as you well know. Sole inheritor of the family fortune. So tell me about this Lorrie, who owns this old house you're so ga-ga about."

Against her will, Holly felt her face turn red. She cleared her throat.

"Still have a crush on him?"

"I have no idea what you mean, " Holly said stiffly.

Taylor glanced toward the door and lowered her voice to a whisper. "Come on, Holly, do you think no one knew where you were that whole summer?"

Holly could only blink at her stepsister.

"I remember that summer because that's when I first met Charles. He was married then, but I knew as soon as I saw him that someday he'd be mine. You were young, but I wanted to tell you that I'd met the man I was going to marry, but when I tried to talk to you, you heard nothing."

"So you snooped?" Holly said, beginning to feel angry. All these years she'd thought that her summer with Lorrie had been her own secret.

"Just taking care of my little sister. Don't worry, the parents know nothing about anything." Taylor leaned back in her chair. "Look, count your blessings. At least they'll approve of this Lorrie. With me, Mom adores Charles and his illustrious ancestors, but Dad says that being a turncoat is in his blood. I think he expects Charles to leave me at the altar."

Holly said nothing, but she didn't care for Taylor's fiancé.

When they'd met, he'd been thirty and married, while Taylor had only been twenty years old. Taylor had never said, but Holly was sure they'd been lovers. Now it was eleven years later and it wasn't as though Taylor had waited for him, but part of Holly felt she had. Was Charles going to prove worth the wait?

"Don't look at me like that," Taylor said. "Don't put that look of pity on your face. 'Poor Taylor. All the men she's turned down while she's waited for Charles's crazy old wife to die.' As you well know, I've just never liked any other man as well as I've liked Charles."

"You've never given any man a chance. What's your record? Four months? As soon as a man starts getting serious about you, you run away."

"My problem is that I regress. I tend to like men like my father."

Holly knew what that meant: big, gorgeous daredevils with no education, no money. Taylor liked men who wore tool belts and carried chain saws. But they weren't the kind of men she could bring home, and she too well remembered her life of poverty before her mother married James Latham.

"Speaking of hunks," Holly said, "I need to look my best for Saturday. I have a dress, but I need–" She touched her hair, then held up her hands in surrender.

"Come upstairs with me and we'll make some appointments. I'll show you what can be done in three days."

# Chapter Seven

Holly sat at the dressing table (Edwardian, inlaid walnut) in her bedroom and tried to still her nervous stomach. In less than an hour she was going to see Lorrie again. Had he changed much, she wondered?

Closing her eyes for a moment, she tried to remember that summer, remember the way she felt. Never since had she admired a person as much as she admired Lorrie that summer. What sixteen-year-old boy would give up a summer of play to repair an old house? Day after day, he'd worked beside Holly as they scraped and repainted. He'd helped her up ladders, had showed her how to carry one end of heavy beams. When she'd pulled back weeds around the dairy and surprised a cottonmouth snake, it had been Lorrie who'd run to the house, got his .22 rifle, and killed the snake. Holly had used the moment to briefly clasp Lorrie about the waist and express her eternal gratitude.

As Holly put on lipstick (the third shade she'd tried), she halted. The problem with trying to remember every moment of her summer with Lorrie was that Nick Taggert's face kept coming into her mind.

"Adulthood!" Holly said in disgust, applied the lipstick, looked at it, then wiped it off.

The problem was that now that she was an adult, it was difficult to sustain a sense of desire for a boy she'd done no more with than work. Every time she thought of Lorrie, Nick's face popped up. When she remembered her fear of the snake, and the way she'd held absolutely still, and the way Lorrie looked behind the rifle, she saw Nick's face. In her mind's eye, she saw Nick shoot the snake, then she saw herself fall on him in gratitude, and she saw them making love on the mown grass near the dairy.

For the last three days she'd rarely been home. Instead, she'd been in Edenton going from one beauty appointment to another. Taylor had always been the hedonist while Holly had been the worker. If the vegetable patch needed weeding, Holly would weed it. Taylor wouldn't have noticed, but if she had, she wouldn't have messed up her perfect manicure to pull weeds.

To get ready to see Lorrie again, Holly had massages, had subtle streaks of color put in her hair, had a facial, most of her body waxed, and a manicure and a pedicure.

By the end of three days she didn't know when she'd ever

been so exhausted. She was dying to get this first meeting over. As she was under the dryer, hot lights beating down on the foil on her head, she hoped Lorrie would take one look at her, ask her to marry him, and then elope with her so she could start work on Belle Chere within a week. When the manicurist gouged her with a nail file, Holly changed the week to four days.

"Ready?" Taylor asked as she walked through the bathroom into Holly's bedroom.

"I think so," Holly said, standing up. She was wearing black hose and a black lace teddy.

Taylor eyed her stepsister critically from head to toe. "You *do* look great."

"You sound as though you wish I didn't," Holly said, smiling, but Taylor didn't laugh.

"You have everything," Taylor said softly.

As always, Holly immediately felt guilty. She put her arm around Taylor's shoulders. "You don't have to worry. You won't end up living in a cold-water flat." Holly tried to make a joke but it fell flat. Taylor's biggest fear in life was that she'd end up like her mother had been: single and broke. Holly suspected that the main reason Taylor was marrying Charles was for the security his old name and his wealth would give her.

When Holly turned twenty-one and had come into her inheritance, the first thing she'd done was set up trusts for the people she loved. For all that her father was well known, he had no real income, nor did his wife. Holly had provided life-time incomes for the three of them. Even if Marguerite divorced Holly's father she'd still have an income as long as she lived. And if Taylor ran off with the lawnmower boy and James disowned her (a distinct possibility), she'd still be able to live well. Not lavishly, but comfortably.

However, Holly still felt guilty whenever Taylor made a reference to the fact that Holly had it all: beauty, wealth, and her father's illustrious name.

Holly wanted to lighten the moment. She went to the armoire (no closets in her bedroom) and pulled out her black silk dress. "So tell me, after one of these one-night stands, how long does it take before you stop seeing the man's face everywhere?"

"Face?" Taylor asked. "They have faces?"

Holly laughed as she stepped into her dress. Her hair had been moussed and sprayed into a perfectly arranged helmet that she didn't dare mess up. "No, really. You must have liked at least one of them."

Taylor sat down on the edge of Holly's bed (built in 1792 and restored by Holly) and stared at her stepsister. "So tell me everything about this man."

"You mean . . . ?" Holly trailed off.

"I'm not interested in your sex life. I have my own very active sex life."

"Really?" Holly asked, turning so Taylor could zip her dress up. "With Charles, I assume."

When Taylor snorted as though to say she couldn't believe Holly could be so naïve, Holly looked at her sharply. "But— who? Taylor, you can't be serious. Charles is—"

"Dear little sister, join the twenty-first century. There are people who need more than an old house to give them an orgasm."

"I don't—" Holly began but stopped. The truth was, she didn't want to hear about whatever Taylor was up to. She was afraid that if she knew, the next time she saw Charles her red face would tell too much.

"Did he make you laugh?" Taylor asked.

"Charles?" Holly asked. "Not— Oh, you mean *him.*" She looked away. The views outside her window were beautiful. She looked over the top of fruit trees to the river beyond. "Yes, he made me laugh. And he got me access into some old houses that—"

"Oh, Lord!" Taylor said. "Call the caterer and book the church. If he got you inside a bunch of old houses, then he found the key to your heart." She got up and went to stand in front of her stepsister. "Were any of those houses as good as Belle Chere?"

"Not hardly," Holly said, smiling.

"So go for the big prize, not the little one. Use all your feminine wiles on Lorrie tonight, make him fall madly in love with you, and you'll get to remodel a whole bunch of old buildings."

"Renovate, not remodel," Holly said without thinking.

"Whatever. Now are you ready to go?"

Holly took a deep breath. "I think so. Wish me luck."

"With your face and body and that dress, you don't need luck. I was thinking. Maybe I should get breast implants."

"Sure," Holly said. "Double Ds at least."

Laughing, they went downstairs.

Spring Hill, built in 1790, had a center hall floor plan. Upstairs and down, a wide center hall went from front to back, with four rooms on each floor leading off the hall. Downstairs was a kitchen, dining room, a sitting room, and a library. A powder room had been stuck under the stairs.

Upstairs, on the right of the hall was the master suite, which consisted of two bedrooms with a connecting door, and two bathrooms. "My own bath helps me keep a sense of mystery," Marguerite had once said.

Across the center hall was one bedroom that shared a bath, a laundry room, and a small sitting room.

It was a simple house with large, gracious rooms. The downstairs rooms had wainscoting on the walls, and deep molding around the doors and ceiling.

Downstairs, James Latham admired his two daughters, offered each his arm, and walked them to the big double front doors. "Had I known there were two such beautiful young women under all that dreadful denim, I'd have stayed home and kept you to myself."

As many times as she'd heard the joke, Holly still smiled. This was the father she knew and loved. He knew how to make women feel beautiful. Growing up, Holly had rarely seen the "other" James Latham, the man who was known as the "hard-nosed negotiator." Since his heart attack, his family was seeing that man more and more often.

Laughing, Holly hugged her father's arm and smiled across his deep chest at Taylor. All was right with the world! She was going to see the man she'd dreamed about for eleven long years. And she was again going to see Belle Chere, beautiful, breathtaking, unpolluted Belle Chere.

Still smiling, looking up at her father, she saw Taylor's face change when the doors were opened. Taylor's eyes darkened, her lashes lowered, and her nostrils flared.

Holly chuckled to herself. Only a man could make a woman look like that and it was no doubt the new gardener who was doing it. Her father no longer had a full-time valet or a dedicated driver, so the two male employees he did have did double duty. Taylor had mentioned that the gardener would be driving them to Belle Chere.

Smiling, Holly turned—and looked into the dark blue eyes of Nick Taggert.

She froze. She stood planted where she was, unable to move forward.

Her father looked at her in puzzlement. "I thought you'd seen the new car," he said. "It isn't a limo. It's a–" He looked at Taylor in question.

"It's an SUV," she said loudly, her eyes on Nick, who was looking at James, carefully not looking at either woman.

"Oh, yes," James said. "An SUV. Holly, it has a television inside it. Come on, let me show you."

Leaving the women behind, he went forward to his newest toy, and Nick opened a sliding door for him.

Holly was still rooted in place, still staring.

"I told you," Taylor whispered. "Isn't he divine?"

Holly tried to breathe. "You're sleeping with him?"

"Not yet, but I'm working on it. He's to be my last fling before I settle into wifehood and joining the garden club." She laughed. "He's going to be *my* gardener." She went forward to get into the car beside her stepfather, and Marguerite followed.

When the three of them were in the big vehicle, they turned to look at Holly, who hadn't moved an inch from the doorway.

"Come on, dear, we'll be late," Marguerite said.

Holly couldn't take her eyes off Nick, but he hadn't looked at her. As though he were a robot, he stood by the sliding door, ready to close it after Holly got inside.

"Wait a minute," James said, looking at Nick. "My daughter becomes ill if she sits in the back. Let her sit in the front with you."

Obediently, Nick slid the door shut, then opened the front passenger door. But Holly still didn't move.

Taylor leaned across her mother and shouted, "Old house! Falling down! Needs rescue!"

They all laughed when the words acted like a dash of cold water on Holly. She shook her head, then slowly walked across the porch and down the steps. When she stood in front of Nick, he still didn't meet her eyes. It was as though he'd never seen her before and was just doing his job.

Maybe he's a look-alike, she thought. Maybe he's like one of those actors who look like famous people and– "Eeek!" Holly squealed because, as she stepped up into the passenger seat, Nick had run a caressing hand over the curve of her behind.

"Are you all right?" Marguerite asked as Nick walked to the other side of the big car.

"Yes," Holly said, swallowing. "I, uh, twisted my ankle."

She looked straight ahead as Nick took the driver's seat and slowly drove down the long gravel drive to the paved road. By water, Belle Chere was very close, but by road, it was about four miles.

Holly desperately wanted to talk to Nick. No, she wanted to scream at him, to demand to know what he thought he was doing there. She wanted to plead with him to leave, and to reason with him by saying that his presence could mess up her entire future. Her maybe future, that is.

The drive to Belle Chere seemed to go on forever. They seemed to pass houses so slowly she began to count windowpanes. She noticed every door frame, every porch post.

"Why are you here?" she hissed at Nick when she heard laughter in the back.

Nick glanced in the rearview mirror and didn't answer. When Holly looked back, Taylor was staring at him.

Holly looked back out the window and tried to calm down. Okay, she could handle this. She was an adult. She just first had to find out what he wanted from her.

When they passed a truck with Hollander Tools printed on the side, she gasped. Had he found out about her inheritance? Was he here to blackmail her?

Blackmail her to whom? If he told her father about them, James would say, "I'm disappointed in your taste in men, Hollander," but he wouldn't really be angry.

Did Nick have photos? Who would care if they were printed? Before her father's retirement, photos of a naked daughter might have caused problems, but not now.

Holly glanced at Nick, but she could read nothing from his profile. What did he want from her? To tell Lorrie of their tryst? To prevent her from possibly dating Lorrie?

Or was he just a stalker? An old-fashioned psycho who had somehow found out where Holly was living and was now out to . . . to. . . . She didn't want to remember any of the horrible things she'd read of what deranged people had done.

She wanted to think more, but Nick turned into the magnificent drive down to Belle Chere. Over a hundred years ago, a double row of oak tress had been planted along the long drive. This had once been common in grand houses, but most of the avenues were now gone. Trees had been cut for their lumber, and trees had been removed when gardens had been plowed to be used for farmland.

Because Belle Chere had been owned by the same family for generations, these oaks had been cared for. When one died, it had been replaced, so that now the avenue was as beautiful as it had been a hundred years ago.

"Oh," Holly said, leaning forward to see upward through the windshield.

Without a word, Nick opened the big sunroof. With a smile, Holly stood up, sticking her head up through the skylight to look and feel the beautiful drive to the house.

When Belle Chere came into view, Nick stopped the car and Holly stood there for a moment looking at the house. "Faded glory" and "majestic lady" were words that came to her.

The house was three stories with wide, double porches across the front. It wasn't that the house was unique; there were still many plantation houses like it. It was that the house was so untouched. In the 1920s one of Lorrie's father's ancestors had converted the smaller parlor in the back into a kitchen. Two full baths and a powder room had been added to the house.

But paneling, carved fireplace surrounds, wall murals, and in some places even wallpaper hadn't been touched in a hundred years.

Holly didn't know how long she stood there, but Taylor tugged on her dress and she looked down.

"Some of us are hungry for more than an old house," Taylor said.

Holly knew this was meant to be an inside joke between her and her stepsister, but when Holly looked down she saw the top of Nick's head. With all her heart she wanted to tell him to stand beside her and look at the house. But Taylor was making jokes about being hungry for Nick . . .

Sitting down, Holly murmured an apology to her family for taking their time.

Nick parked the van at the side of the house, then silently and perfectly, as though he'd always done it, opened the door and helped everyone out. When it was Holly's turn her heart began to pound rapidly. If she hadn't had on a long dress and high heels she would have leaped to the ground, but when she tried to get out on her own, her heel caught in her hem.

The next thing she knew, Nick's hands were on her waist and she was being lifted from the seat and swung through the air. He stood her on the ground, still never meeting her eyes, then went back to close the car doors.

"I'll have to try that next time," Taylor whispered.

James said, "That boy is a better driver than a gardener."

Holly said nothing. She kept her shoulders back and her eyes straight ahead as her father banged the big brass knocker. She was about to see Lorrie again!

# Chapter Eight

From the first second she looked at Lorrie, Holly knew she'd done the right thing in manipulating her family so she could be near him and Belle Chere.

He was tall, handsome, with dark blond, wavy hair and beautiful brown eyes. He was dressed in a dark suit, proper evening attire, and he was charming.

"Hollander," he said softly, taking her shoulders in his hands, "you grew up." With sparkling eyes, he looked at her family. "Did she tell you of our summer together?"

"Not a word," Taylor said. "But we'd love to hear all about it."

Yes, Holly thought, so would I. How had he seen their summer together?

"She was the best buddy a boy could have," Lorrie said, smiling and showing the perfect teeth she remembered so well.

"Buddy?" Taylor said under her breath, making Holly frown.

"Would you like to see the house?" Lorrie asked. "And perhaps Holly would like to lead the tour since she knows it so well."

"No!" James, Marguerite, and Taylor said in unison.

Lorrie looked at Holly with a questioning look and in spite of her low-cut dress that showed too much of her ample bosom, she felt as though she were again thirteen years old. "I tend to get too technical," she said.

"My daughter's love of old houses makes her verbose," James said, then glanced toward an open doorway to the left. "If you don't mind, young man, I'll forego the tour for a little single malt."

"I'd kill for a glass of wine," Taylor said.

"You wouldn't have any sherry, would you?" Marguerite asked.

Lorrie gave Holly a shrug, as though to say, What am I to do? then ushered her family into the sitting room. He blocked Holly's entrance.

"Hey, kiddo," he said softly, his voice quiet so only she could hear him, "you really did grow up." He pointedly looked down her dress. "Did you know how, uh, difficult that summer was for me? You were one cute little kid."

Holly's joy at hearing those words nearly made her swoon on her feet. Ask me to marry you and I'll take the front bedroom, she wanted to yell. But she said nothing.

Lorrie glanced over his shoulder at the three people helping themselves to the drinks table, then put his hand up to tuck a curl behind Holly's ear. But thanks to three kinds of "superhold" concoctions, he couldn't bend her hair. For a second, he looked fascinated by this and Holly thought he might be going to use both hands on her stiffened hair.

When she stepped back, he dropped his hand, but he still kept looking at her hair in puzzlement.

"I know you want to see the house, so go ahead. I'll cover for you."

Holly didn't even consider being polite. One second she was in the hall and the next she was halfway up the central stairs, heading toward the bedrooms. What had been done in eleven years? Any changes made?

She got to the top of the landing and halted. Before her were five closed doorways that led into the bedrooms. How much had been changed since she last saw them? Two bathrooms used to have pull-chain toilets. Had that changed? Half the window frames had been rotten eleven years ago. Had they been replaced? How bad was the plasterwork ceiling in the big blue bedroom?

Her hand was on the newel post (solid mahogany), but her feet weren't moving. Below her, she could hear laughter and the clink of glassware.

There was business she had to take care of now, she thought, business that couldn't wait, and that was Nick Taggert. Grimacing, cursing him for ruining her first night in the wonderful old house, she tiptoed down the stairs. Since her heels were so high, that wasn't easy, but she managed to do it. "If my arches fall because of you, Nick Taggert . . ." she muttered.

Downstairs, she paused and glanced into the sitting room and saw everyone smiling at Lorrie. Even her father was smiling and this warmed Holly. Her father never smiled at Taylor's fiancé.

"Better and better," Holly murmured. Everyone liked the man she liked. The only problem now was Nick Taggert. All she had to do was get rid of him and all obstacles would be out of her way. By the end of the summer—no, she thought—by Christmas she planned to be mistress of Belle Chere.

And married to Lorrie, she added.

By the time she got outside, her temper was at the boiling point. She was *not* going to allow some redneck who she'd had a brief fling with ruin her life!

She ran across the lawn to the van, but Nick wasn't there. "Nick!" she hissed. She could see inside the house, saw her family still laughing and Lorrie pouring drinks from a pitcher. If Holly weren't running around outside with the mosquitoes, she could have been inside sipping something cold and lethal, and inspecting the condition of the ceiling molding.

Angrily, she hiked her dress up to her knees and ran down the path to the dairy. No Nick. However, the dairy looked to be in good condition.

Hissing "Nick" now and then, she hurried to the icehouse. Empty. She went across the lawn to the old office. It was locked and looked as though the roof needed work.

There was no one there. Sweat coated her body.

I should go inside *now,* she thought, gently wiping her face, trying not to mess up her makeup. I can talk to the man tomorrow. I can—

She broke off because she saw a shadow move through the *parterres*—the big, boxed-in gardens that had once been so beautiful. In the middle of the first two had been marble fountains. Maybe she should just glance at them and see if the fountains were all right.

Hiking up her skirt again, but walking sedately so she didn't sweat more, she went down the crunchy gravel path toward the garden.

Nick was standing by a marble fountain of a little boy. Holly knew there were two fountains, one on each side, and they were of two little boys, brothers, who'd both died in a boating accident in 1821. Their bereaved parents had the fountains carved in Italy and sent to Belle Chere.

Holly walked toward Nick, ready to have it out with him, but something happened as she looked at him. The moonlight fell over him, turning his dark hair a silvery blue. Shadows were cast over his broad shoulders and down his long legs.

Her step quickened and when it did, the sweat began to trickle down between her breasts.

When Nick turned and saw her, Holly began to run. When Nick smiled at her, she ran faster. When he opened his arms to her, she leaped over the boxwood hedge and when she nearly fell, he caught her.

His lips were on hers in a second and in the next she was backed up against the fountain, her skirt around her waist. Deftly, Nick unsnapped the crotch of her teddy, her pantyhose tore—and he was in her.

She threw a leg around his hip, his hands were on her bottom, and he drove into her. She felt as though she were starving and only this man could feed her. She clawed at him as she pulled him closer and closer, as she rose to meet his every thrust in a frenzy of need and desire.

When he came, she was with him, and she collapsed against him. Nick pulled her up until both her legs were around his hips and he held her to him.

Holly buried her face in his sweaty neck and hugged him with both arms and both legs. And this hugging was almost more intimate than what they'd just done.

Oh, heavens, but she'd *missed* him, she thought. She hated to think that, to *know* that, but she had missed him.

"You can't stay here," she whispered into his neck.

"Sssh," he said, then put his hand on her hair. "What the— Ow! I think your hair just cut my hand."

"Very funny," she said, but she laughed—and when she did, he came out of her.

"Uh-oh," Nick said, kissing her neck. "Why don't we go–"

That sobered her. She got off his body and tried to regain her dignity–which was impossible under the circumstances. Her hose were torn and she could feel them starting to move down. Her teddy was unsnapped and it was inching upward. Also, she realized that this was the second time they'd had unprotected sex. The first time was in her car and now tonight.

Standing in front of him, pressed up against a marble fountain of a tragically killed child, it was all too much for Holly. "You have to leave here," she said, close to tears. "You can't stay. I have plans for my life that don't include you."

Once he'd fastened his trousers, Nick stepped back and gestured toward the house. "You're free. I haven't interfered and I won't. Your life is your own."

She took a breath. "Why are you here?"

"For the job, of course."

She put both hands over her face, tried to calm herself, then looked back at him. They both knew he was lying. He'd come there for her. "Okay, so I'm attracted to you. We've proven that. But then, so are lots of women attracted to you. Taylor is going crazy over you."

"Too skinny. Too aggressive," he said. "I like my women–"

When he reached out to her, she stepped back. "Nick! I am not your woman and never will be. Look, I can get you another job. You can work for someone a lot better tempered than my father. You'll make more money. You'll–"

"No thanks," he said, putting his hands in his pockets. "I like it here and your dad's okay. He spent about an hour today explaining what really happened at the Bay of Pigs invasion. Interesting man."

Holly opened her mouth to speak, but couldn't. She'd thought that she could get her father to fire him, but if Nick was listening to and enjoying her father's stories, there was no hope Nick would be discharged.

"Italy!" Holly said. "How'd you like to work there? Sunshine and olives."

"Nope."

She leaned back against the fountain. "Why are you doing this to me? You must have gone to a lot of trouble to find out my father needed help. Why?"

Nick looked up at the moon for a moment, then back at her. "Curiosity maybe. I wanted to find out some things."

"Please tell me you aren't in love with me."

"I don't think so." He looked at her breasts. "Lust, yeah, but not love."

Part of Holly didn't like that. But then, didn't every woman want every man to declare love for her?

She straightened her shoulders and smoothed her skirt. She'd need privacy to fix the mess her undergarments were in. "This won't happen again. This was–" She couldn't meet his eyes.

"So this guy's already asked you to marry him?"

"Of course not. Tonight's the first time I've seen him."

"Then what's the problem? Your sister's planning her wedding, but she's been hanging around the tool shed and making me propositions that you wouldn't believe. She–"

"Careful!" Holly said. "I won't listen to any disparagement of my sister."

"The point is that you're not going with anybody, you're not engaged or married, and you're an adult, so why not fool around with the lawnmower boy? Maybe I could give you some pointers about how to reel ol' Lorrie and his mansion in."

In spite of her common sense, Holly was intrigued by this statement. "Such as?"

Nick shrugged. "Men talk. I could share what I hear with you."

"No offense, but I doubt if Lorrie is going to tell his most intimate secrets to someone who cuts the neighbor's grass."

"So fix it so I'm around him."

"I can't–" Holly began, then narrowed her eyes at him. "Why would you do that for me? What's your *real* motive?"

"If you marry him, who manages all the restoration of this place? Who gets a salary plus free housing, homegrown veggies, and a bonus at Christmas? I figure it might as well be me as the next guy."

"But you and I– We . . ."

"I'll get a wife, have half a dozen kids, you marry this guy, have two perfect little children, and we'll laugh about it all someday. We'll say, remember the day we met at the fountain?"

Holly was sure there was a flaw in his reasoning, but at the moment she couldn't see it. She wanted to go back to the house, get into the nearest bathroom, and clean herself up. She wanted to see Belle Chere, wanted to have about three strong, cold drinks, and stop thinking.

"Blackmailing you would get me in jail and cut me out of a great future," he said, reading her mind. "Stop worrying so much."

When he reached out to touch her cheek, she pulled back. Nick dropped his hand. "I'll make you a deal. I'll not so much as touch your hand unless *you* start it. You stay away from me and I won't touch you. Deal?"

"I . . ." She didn't know what to say. Through the trees she heard a door open, then Taylor called, "Holly?"

"I have to go. I have to—" She flung her arms around his neck and kissed him. "I hate you," she whispered. "Coming here was a despicable thing to do to me."

"It was," he said, kissing her neck. "Despicable." He pushed her away. "Go before I'm stuck in a ménage à trois."

"Disgusting!" she whispered as she hiked up her gown and ran toward the house.

# Chapter Nine

THIRTY MINUTES AFTER SHE LEFT NICK, HOLLY was seated at Lorrie's dining table. The table had been in his family since the 1760s, when it had been commissioned by his family in England. It had nicks and scars on it—and she knew that Lorrie knew the story behind each imperfection.

There had been an awkward moment when Holly had appeared in the sitting room. She'd done her best to repair herself. She'd had to discard her torn pantyhose, but she'd straightened her underpants and snapped her teddy into place. Her hair and makeup had been a disaster. Between her sweat, Nick's sweat, and his many kisses, all she had left was a bit of eyeliner at the corners of her eyes. In spite of all the products she'd used, her hair was flat to her head.

Searching through the old bathroom cabinet (which needed to be replaced), she found a comb painted with daisies, circa 1970, and managed to get the tangles out. Soap and water was all she could do with her face.

Sheepishly, she'd presented herself in the sitting room. Her stepmother looked at her in chagrin, her father frowned, and Taylor looked at Holly in speculation, as though trying to figure out what she'd been up to.

Lorrie, however, began to laugh as he walked toward her. "So how does my home look?" he asked.

"The roof on the office looks bad. It was dark, but I think I saw some dry rot."

Still laughing, Lorrie put his arm around her shoulders. "Now that's the Holly I remember: She can spot dry rot even in the moonlight."

Holly couldn't keep from blushing. Lorrie thought she'd been outside looking at the buildings when the truth was she'd been outside . . . She gave a weak smile at her family, who seemed to be thinking that they couldn't believe there were two people like her on earth.

Lorrie poured Holly a drink, which she gulped, then he ushered them all into dinner. Immediately, James's face fell. Obviously, he'd been expecting a proper dinner, with courses, something homemade and delicious. Instead, he was faced with what looked like Kentucky Fried Chicken. The food was served on hundred-year-old china and there were goblets of paper-thin glass, but the food was commercial and ordinary.

"As you can see, I haven't been back long enough to hire a

cook," Lorrie said, but he didn't seem to be embarrassed.

He sat at one end of the table, James at the other, the three women in between. As soon as they sat down, Holly began talking. She said she hadn't seen the orchard, hadn't seen the family cemetery, and what were the conditions of the stables and the coach house? How was the barn? Was the sawmill intact? Did the blacksmith shop still have the bellows or had the leather rotted? Did—?

Smiling, Lorrie interrupted her. "My dear Holly, I think the other guests are bored to death. Perhaps we could talk of something besides Belle Chere."

"Yes, of course," Holly murmured, looking down at her untouched food.

For about thirty minutes she was silent as she listened to her family interrogate Lorrie. She well knew that they were trying to figure out if he was "suitable" for Holly. If all of what was being said hadn't been so important to her, she would have changed the subject.

But Lorrie could handle his own. In answering the questions, he quickly skipped over his recent divorce, smiling and making jokes about what had to have been a painful time. He said that after it was done all he'd wanted was to return home to Belle Chere. When he said he was going to open a law practice in Edenton, Holly looked at him sharply.

"You'll be in town a lot then?" When everyone looked at her, she looked at her plate.

"All right," Taylor said loudly, "this pussyfooting around has to stop. Lorric, Holly is leading up to asking you if she can spend the summer digging around in your attic and reading all your old papers. She wants to do her Ph.D. dissertation on the history of this house. May she?"

"Of course," Lorrie said. "I'd be honored and pleased to have written documentation of my family's sometimes infamous history. Maybe she can find the family treasure."

The word "treasure" effectively halted all of them.

"Infamous?" Holly asked. "Since when has anyone connected to Belle Chere been infamous?"

Lorrie leaned back in his chair. He'd eaten very little. "I never told you the story because I didn't know it until a few years ago. My father considered his ancestor, Arthur Beaumont, someone not to be spoken of. Considering my father . . ." Lorrie trailed off, and the women looked away. Lorrie's father had been involved in too many nefarious activities to look down on anyone.

"So what about a treasure?" James asked. "This place looks like it could use some treasure."

Holly gasped at the rudeness of her father's words, but Lorrie laughed. "It could use all of Blackbeard's loot," he said. "Shall we adjourn to the sitting room? I have some brandy we could—"

"Did you buy it at the local grocery?" James asked.

"No, sir, my great-great-great-grandfather risked the lives

of half a dozen slaves to take it from a French ship that went aground. Would you like to try it?"

"I might be persuaded," James said as he left the table.

In the sitting room, Lorrie lit candles and poured big snifters (old and terrifyingly fragile) full of brandy and they settled down to hear his story.

"It's an old story," Lorrie began. "Two brothers were in love with the same young lady, a Miss Julia Bayard Pemberton."

"Spring Hill," Holly said.

"Yes, she lived at your house." Lorrie raised his snifter in salute to her memory. "It was told to me that Julia had been in love with my ancestor, the handsome, charismatic Jason Beaumont, since they were children. But Jason's father died when Jason was only sixteen, and in grief the young man ran off to sea."

He paused to take a sip of brandy. "At least that's the official story. I think the truth was that his older brother, Arthur, made Jason's life such a living hell that he ran away from home. My great-aunt, who told me all the parts of the story my father left out, said that Arthur was as homely as Jason was handsome, as unlikable as Jason was adored by all."

"But he was the oldest so he inherited Belle Chere," Holly said softly, for the Beaumont family followed the English custom of leaving everything to the eldest son and nothing to the other children. Younger sons were given a token allowance and daughters were expected to marry well.

"Yes," Lorrie said. "Arthur received everything at his father's death, but in an unusual gesture, Jason was given the right to live at Belle Chere for his lifetime. There used to be a house that was said to have been built for him. I think it was west of the stables."

"Near the big maple trees," Holly said.

"Yes." Lorrie smiled at her in a way that made her look away, pleased at his look of praise. "So Jason ran away to sea and didn't return for ten long years. He returned in, I think it was 1843 or '44, and when he returned, he found Julia engaged to marry Arthur."

"She wanted Belle Chere," Holly said.

"Maybe, but when Jason returned, she broke her engagement to Arthur and announced she was going to marry the younger, more handsome Beaumont."

"Yeow!" Taylor said. "Was there a duel?"

"No. In fact, Arthur was gracious about it. He threw the two of them a huge party and laughed about everything."

"He was lying," Marguerite said softly. "He was covering a cold and very deep rage."

The others looked at her, but Marguerite kept her eyes on Lorrie.

"A week before the wedding was to take place, Jason had an argument with the owner of the local cotton gin and that night the man and his wife were shot dead. Four witnesses said they saw Jason Beaumont do it. But Jason said he'd been at home all that night playing cards with his brother Arthur."

Lorrie paused to sip his brandy, obviously enjoying the looks of his audience as they waited for the rest of the story.

"When the sheriff and his men came to arrest Jason, he laughed and said his brother could tell them where he'd been all night. But Arthur said he couldn't lie, even for his brother, and that he had no idea where his brother had been that night. They took Jason away in chains, he was tried, found guilty, and hanged for the double murder."

When Lorrie stopped, the others waited.

"What about the treasure?" James snapped.

"Ah yes, the treasure. Those were different times than today. After the trial, Jason asked to be released from jail for twenty-four hours so he could clear up some family matters. He gave his word as a gentleman that he'd return."

"He killed Arthur!" Taylor said.

"Oh no, it was much worse," Lorrie said, smiling.

"Belle Chere," Holly whispered.

"Yes. Belle Chere. Somehow, Jason kept his brother away for a day. First, he married his beloved Julia, who was carrying his child, then he and a trusted servant—isn't there always a trusted servant?—removed every item of wealth from Belle Chere. Jason hauled off wagonloads of silver objects and he emptied the vault—which is still in the basement, by the way—of all the proceeds from the sale of that year's crops. If it had any resale value, Jason took it."

"And hid it," James said.

"Yes. He hid the treasure so well that it's never been found."

"And he took the secret to his death," Marguerite said. "It's horrible what jealousy can cause."

"I believe I remember reading that Julia Bayard Pemberton married Arthur Beaumont," Holly said.

"Right again. Jason was hardly cold when Julia married Arthur, and seven months later, she gave birth to a son who looked very much like Jason."

"I understand why she married Arthur," Taylor said. "If she was pregnant, she needed a husband, but why did Arthur marry her? After all, she'd publically humiliated him."

"Did I mention that Jason, along with being handsome, was also a cousin to Midas? My great-aunt said that Jason could buy a dying company and it would revive. At the time of his death he was a very wealthy man."

"Belle Chere," Holly said again. "Arthur no longer had the money to keep Belle Chere going so he married his brother's widow so he could use his brother's money to keep the place."

"That poor child," Marguerite said. "How Arthur must have hated Julia and Jason's child."

"He never saw him," Lorrie said. "A few months after his brother was hanged, Arthur fell off his horse, broke his neck, and died. Julia's son inherited everything and did an excellent job of keeping the Yankees from burning the place to the ground."

For a few moments the five of them sat there, sipping the wonderful old brandy and thinking about the story.

"The artifacts have never been found, none of them?" James asked.

"No. When part of the icehouse collapsed in the seventies, we found the silver service—what you ate with tonight—that my family hid from the Yankees, but we never found the big hoard, what Jason hid."

"And the servant?" Holly asked. "What happened to him? He must have known where the treasure was hidden."

"We don't know what happened to him. My great-aunt said she'd been told that the man was supposed to have told Julia where it was buried, but he didn't."

"Probably took it himself," Taylor said, finishing her brandy. "After poor ol' Jason was hanged, Faithful probably went back to wherever and took everything."

"Maybe, but I don't think so. The night after Jason was hanged, one of the four witnesses got drunk and was cursing Arthur Beaumont for not paying his debts. The next day he was found floating facedown in the river. Within hours, everyone in town put the story together and realized Jason had probably been innocent. However, since in those days Belle Chere was too rich to disparage, no one said anything. My great-aunt said that Arthur threatened death to the house slaves if it got out that Jason had stolen everything. Arthur was able to suppress the whole story so it never became local legend.

"As for the hiding place having been emptied, all I can say is that my great-aunt assures me that it's never been found."

Lorrie took a breath. "Anyway, I think that if anything suspicious had happened then, such as a slave suddenly becoming wealthy, the town would have questioned why."

"And there would have been another lynching of an innocent man," Holly said.

"Probably."

James was looking at Lorrie in speculation. "You said that this story isn't usually told in your family. So why are you telling *us* now?"

"Caught," Lorrie said, setting down his empty brandy glass. "When the local gossip was that you'd bought Spring Hill and that all your family was returning here, I formed a devious, underhanded plot to try to persuade Holly to help me look for the treasure. All I know is that it's on this property somewhere." He looked at Holly, his eyes darkening, his lashes lowered. "Could I persuade you to help me search?"

Holly restrained herself enough to keep from jumping up and dancing about the room. "Yes, I think I could do that," she said, as though contemplating the matter. When the others burst into laughter, not at all fooled by her apparent reticence, Holly laughed, too.

"I'll split it with you," Lorrie said.

Holly wanted to say, You mean like in community property? but she didn't. "My reward will be in writing a dissertation that gets me my doctorate. Instead of writing the whole history of the house, I'll write the true story of Arthur, Jason, and Julia, and I'll end it all with photos of pre–Civil War artifacts I found hidden."

"If anyone can do it, it will be you," Lorrie said, looking at her so hotly that a little trickle of sweat ran down the back of Holly's neck.

"Shall we start tomorrow?" Holly asked. Lorrie and Belle Chere. Life was good.

"Oh," Lorrie said, "there's a problem. I'm afraid I have commitments in town. I have a lot of work to do to set up my new law practice. There isn't enough work in Edenton, so I have to make my former clients believe that I'm willing to go where they are." He shrugged. "Living out of a suitcase is a price I'll have to pay to be able to take care of Belle Chere. In fact, I have to go to New York tomorrow."

"That's all right," Holly said. "I know where the attic is. I'll just–"

"Stay here all day alone?" James said. "Over my dead body. I'll send that lawn boy to stay with you. He looks strong enough to protect you and heaven knows he's a terrible gardener. He cut the daffodil leaves down yesterday. I doubt if they'll bloom next year."

"I think it would be safe for Holly to stay here during the day," Lorrie said. "I don't see the need for an escort."

"Humph!" James said. "Last week we got a call from the

police saying they suspected she'd been kidnapped. All of us went through hours of hell before we heard she was safe. You know what happened to her? She was wandering around inside one of those rotten old houses she loves so much, saw a rattlesnake–yes! a rattler–and fell into a concrete-lined pit. It was only by chance that some trucker found her and got her out before she died of exposure."

His eyes bore into Lorrie's. "I know that you two revere this place, but the truth is that every other board is probably being held up by termites holding hands, and I can tell you that when it comes to old houses, my daughter has no sense at all. What if she fell through the attic floor or got herself locked in your vault? What if a ceiling fell on her? With you gone and with us busy, she could go for hours undiscovered. No, if she's here then she isn't to be alone. If it's not to be the gardener who doesn't know a weed from a flower, then who else plans to stay with her? One of you?"

For a moment no one spoke. What James had said was true.

"I think the gardener will do nicely," Marguerite said.

Taylor smiled at Holly and she knew what her stepsister was thinking. She would be visiting Belle Chere to continue her pursuit of the handsome gardener, away from her stepfather's watchful eye.

Holly wanted to protest, but could think of nothing to say, You see, Dad, she could say, I want to *marry* Lorrie, but I keep having sex with the gardener. I'm afraid that if the gardener's around me all the time I'll get caught and that will ruin my chances with Lorrie.

No, she couldn't say that. She was just going to have to rely on her own self-control. Or, better yet, she was going to have to rely on the beauty and mystique of Belle Chere to distract her from the dark good looks of Nick Taggert.

She gave her father a weak smile and she could swear she saw a twinkle in his eyes, as though he was up to something.

In the next second, she grinned. Her father was helping her to reel Lorrie in. If she was there, at his house, alone all day and waiting for him, Lorrie would feel secure. But if she was there with an incredibly handsome and sexy man, maybe Lorrie would return from his trips sooner. Hadn't they just heard a story about the horror that jealousy could cause?

The twinkle in her father's eyes deepened, and Holly looked back at Lorrie. "Yes," she said, "maybe it would be better to have someone with me. He can move boxes about in the attic."

"I find that I'm quite jealous of the gardener," Lorrie said, his eyes boring so hotly into Holly's that for a moment she thought he might be going to say something intimate.

James cleared his throat. "Since that's settled, I suggest we go home. Tomorrow I have a sermon to prepare."

Feeling a bit dazed, Holly followed her family out of the sitting room. For years she'd dreamed of this, dreamed and wondered. She'd been so young when she'd spent a summer with Lorrie, and over the years she'd wondered what kind of man he'd grown into. Sometimes she'd run across people from Edenton and she'd always asked about Lorrie. Everyone knew of his family and the estate of Belle Chere, and nearly everyone claimed to "know" him. Many people had said he was a snob.

But the Lorrie she'd spent the summer with and the man she'd remet again tonight seemed as far removed from being a snob as could be. As an heiress, Holly well knew that you had to be standoffish to people. Too many times, when people had discovered that she was heir to Hollander Tools, they'd changed toward her. Suddenly, their voices were different, and whatever Holly said was outrageously funny or profoundly wise. When she'd fled from these people, she'd later heard that they'd said she was a snob.

As Nick held the door open to the big SUV her father had bought, Holly looked around Belle Chere. There was an age and an elegance to the place that only centuries could attain.

"Are you also the gardener?" she heard Lorrie ask from behind her, then turned to see him frowning. He was looking Nick up and down and didn't seem to like what he saw.

Nick, on the other hand, was smiling at Lorrie in such a superior, "I won" way, that Holly wanted to kick him. "Yes, sir," Nick said. The words were right, but there was a mocking tone in Nick's voice. This is not going to work, Holly thought.

In the next second, Lorrie grabbed her arm, spun her so she was pressed against his body, and kissed her. It was a proper kiss—on the mouth, but with no tongue since her parents were looking on—but Holly was so nervous, what with everyone looking, that she couldn't decide if she liked it or not.

As abruptly as he'd clutched her, Lorrie released her and stepped away. He looked into the back of the car at her father. "Sorry, sir. Moonlight. Old friend who's grown into a beautiful woman." He shrugged in a way that was very appealing.

"Perfectly all right," James said, taking his wife's hand in his. "I've experienced a little moonlight in my lifetime."

Holly started to say something, but Nick put his hands on her waist so tightly she couldn't take a breath. He lifted her, set her down hard in the passenger seat, then shut the door in her face. The next second he was behind the wheel and they were leaving Belle Chere.

Holly wanted to stand up through the sunroof and wave good-bye to Lorrie and to all of Belle Chere, but when she tried to turn, she found that the hem of her dress was caught in the door. She was sure Nick had done it on purpose. When she looked at his profile, she saw a muscle working in his jaw.

Holly turned her head and looked out the window—and smiled. Okay, so she knew she should be angry. Nick had acted in an infantile way. For that matter, so had Lorrie. If he hadn't seen Nick, didn't know that Nick was going to be "guarding" Holly, Lorrie would never have kissed her in front of her parents.

Yes, she should be angry at both men. They were using her in some primitive, male tug-of-war.

But, try as she might, Holly couldn't be mad. It felt too good to have two handsome men fighting over her. Too, too good.

She leaned back against the seat and closed her eyes. Everything was going to her plan. Tomorrow she'd start her research, and if she was lucky, she'd find a treasure that had been hidden for over a hundred and sixty years—a treasure that Belle Chere needed. She hadn't had much time to look around tonight, what with Nick and all (she glanced at him but he was staring straight ahead), but she'd seen several repairs that were needed. Preserving a place like Belle Chere took a fortune. She knew Lorrie had been left no money when he'd inherited Belle Chere, so all he had was what he earned. For all his success as a lawyer, Lorrie was only twenty-seven. He hadn't had enough time to earn the money he needed.

So how grateful would he be to a woman who found the treasure? she wondered. If she found it, it would be Lorrie's and he'd be rich. He'd never be accused of living off his rich wife as she'd heard an old schoolmate of his say about Lorrie's first wife.

Smiling, Holly relaxed against the seat. Yes, everything was working out perfectly to her advantage. It was as though some cupid had planned everything.

Except for Nick, she thought, opening her eyes and looking at his profile. Only her meeting with Nick didn't seem to fit. She needed to figure out a way to get rid of him. Maybe tomorrow she'd call Hollander Tools and see if they had a manager trainee program. If not, she'd strongly suggest that they create one. Yes, she thought, a fabulous job would be the way to get rid of Nick. If she set him up with a job and therefore a future such as he'd never be able to obtain on his own, her conscience would be clear.

Smiling broadly, she was pleased with herself. She had everything figured out.

# Chapter Ten

Holly was sure that the attic of Belle Chere was the hottest place on earth. The windows had long ago been nailed shut, then painted over, and her conscience wouldn't allow her to pry them open. No, the windows would need to be carefully taken out, the paint removed, the frames repaired, then put back into place.

She'd worn her best white linen trousers, cute little flat sandals, and a black cotton sleeveless top. She'd thought that she'd be cool enough, and she'd thought that the research would so absorb her that she'd be able to bear the heat, but it was still morning and she was sweltering.

Yet again, she looked at the big fan at the end of the long, dusty room. How many years since anyone had turned it on? she wondered. From the look of it, it had been new in about 1957. She wasn't surprised to see an old wooden toolbox open beside the fan. It looked as though someone had tried to fix it but had given up and walked away.

She stepped between two horsehide-covered trunks to look out the sealed, dirty window. She could see Nick below, lying in a hammock under an enormous pecan tree, his eyes closed and looking as cool as ice.

This morning he'd been a pain. Because her father had insisted on all of them hearing the first draft of his sermon, Holly hadn't been able to leave the house until 9:00 A.M. She'd been dying to get her hands on the Belle Chere files, but she'd had to wait. When she got away, Nick was sitting on the porch waiting for her.

"Which car will you be wanting, Miss?" he asked.

"Cut it out," she snapped, not looking at him. She was checking the contents of her red leather briefcase to make sure she had all her research materials. Without looking at Nick, she walked to her own car and prepared to get behind the wheel, but Nick brushed her hand away, signaling that he would drive.

They didn't speak during the few minutes it took them to get to Belle Chere. Without looking at him, she used the key Lorrie had given her and opened the front door, leaving Nick outside.

It was as cool in the house as eighteenth-century technology could make it. The central hall was, as they say, "high, wide, and handsome." For a moment, Holly hummed a tune and waltzed about the hall. Parties had been held in the hall. Who designs houses for dancing nowadays? she thought.

She stopped waltzing and decided to go straight up to the attic before it got too hot. But it already was too hot. Centuries-old houses were one thing, but centuries-old air was another.

By 10:30 she was so sweaty she felt as though she'd been swimming. When a bead of sweat dropped off her nose onto an old document, she knew something had to be done. Tomorrow she'd get service people to install a new fan—or a window air conditioner. But for today . . .

She glanced out the dirty window again and saw that Nick was still dozing in the hammock. Maybe she should give him something to do, like change the oil in her car. Rotate the tires. Clean the pistons. Did pistons need cleaning?

Holly stripped off her clothes down to her underwear and sandals. And necklace, she thought in dismay. Since she'd met Nick she'd been wearing the big yellow stone he'd given her. Silly of her to wear something so gaudy and so cheap, but she liked it. There was something about the stone that appealed to her. She'd decided it wasn't glass but was something else, a citrine maybe? She should give the necklace back to him, of course, and she meant to. But for now . . .

She tucked the stone into her bra, turned to an old leather-bound trunk, said, "Show me what ya got!" then opened it.

It was an hour later, when she was stretching on her tiptoes to pull down boxes, that she heard a sound behind her. Turning, she saw Nick and gasped—and when she did, the boxes began to tumble.

In an instant, Nick was behind her, his long arms reaching above her head to push the boxes back up.

Dropping her arms, Holly glared at him. "You're supposed to wait for me downstairs."

He gave her nearly nude body a look up and down. "Nice necklace. I especially like the display case." Turning, he walked toward the fan.

Hastily, Holly shoved the yellow stone back into her bra, but it hurt so she took it out again. No use trying to hide it now. "That's broken," she said as he fiddled with the fan.

Nick examined the fan, then pushed two hatboxes and a moth-eaten teddy bear aside to find the cord. He followed it until it plugged into an extension cord, then he moved at least twenty boxes until he found the plug. Smiling at her, he plugged in the fan and it started blowing dust and papers across the room.

Holly knew she should run after the papers, but the air felt so good she ran to stand in front of the fan, her back to it, arms and legs outstretched.

Nick sat down on an old leather and wood Eastlake chair and watched her. "Wish I had a camera," he murmured.

Holly turned her back to him as she let the fan dry the

sweat on her body. "Not even you can stop me from enjoying this," she said.

"Since when have I tried to stop you from enjoying anything? In fact, I thought part of my job was to give you enjoyment."

She turned back to face him. "Don't start on me—and quit looking at me like that. I have work to do."

"Ah, yes, winning the hand in marriage of Belle Chere."

She glared at him. "You're not at all funny."

"Sometimes I've made you laugh." His voice was low and husky.

"Nick! I mean it! I don't have time to fool around with you."

"What's wrong?" he asked, the smile gone from his face.

She sat down on an old stool and looked around the huge room at all the boxes, trunks, and cabinets. "As far as I can tell, every piece of paper concerning the occupants of Belle Chere since it was built are in this room. But there's no organization, no labeling, no way to find something. Cataloging all this is a year-long job for about twenty graduate students."

Nick was looking at her in puzzlement. "So what's the rush? You can become Mrs. Belle Chere, then spend your life reading these old papers."

"You can be a real jerk, you know that?" She went across the room to her clothes and angrily pulled on her trousers.

Nick got out of the chair. "You're right. I apologize. The

problem is that I don't know what you're trying to do. Do you need to read every piece of paper in here before you can write your dissertation?"

She was buttoning her blouse. Her clothes were dusty and wrinkled, but at least they were now dry. "No," she said, "things have changed. I just need–" She waved her hand. "It's too much to go into." She opened a big armoire, then sighed when she saw the contents: boxes of various ages and states of deterioration, with hundreds of old letters shoved into the empty spaces. She pulled out two letters. "World War One and the Civil War," she said. "How will I find anything quickly?"

Moving behind her, Nick put his hands on her shoulders. She didn't move away. "I have an idea. How about if we go downstairs and you take a shower while I make us some lunch? While we eat you can tell me what to look for, then I'll come up here and help you."

When Holly looked hesitant, Nick said dryly, "I *can* read."

"I . . ." Holly began, but her face turned red.

"I make a mean lemonade," he said.

"In that case . . ." Smiling, she headed for the door, but Nick stopped her. He put his hands at her neck and pulled the necklace he'd given her to outside her blouse. "It looks good," he said softly.

Holly thought he was going to kiss her so she leaned forward, but Nick took her shoulders and turned her toward the door. "You're too sweaty for me!"

"Shall I test that?" Holly said over her shoulder.

"Please don't," he said in such a pleading way that she laughed.

Forty-five minutes later, Holly felt much better. She'd taken a cool shower, washed her hair with Lorrie's shampoo, washed her underwear and hung it on his heated towel bar, and she was now sitting in the kitchen with Nick eating a thick turkey sandwich. She was on her third glass of icy cold lemonade, and she'd just finished telling Nick all she knew of the story of Arthur, Jason, and Julia.

"So you're looking for the 1840s," he said. "But exactly what are you looking for? Julia's diary telling her private story?"

"I wish. I found a Bible that contained some dates but not much else." She started to look in her pocket for her notes, but she was wearing Lorrie's green silk dressing gown. "The dates are right and the facts are there. Everything happened in 1842. The Bible said Julia married Jason on the ninth of April 1842, and three days later he died, but it didn't say how he died. She married Arthur in June and had a baby–" She took a drink of her lemonade.

"Early December," he said.

"Right. How did you know that?" Before he could answer, she said, "Big family."

"Yeah, lots of pregnant women in my family. We Taggerts are very fertile."

"Speaking of which–"

"More lemonade?" he asked, cutting her off. "When did Arthur die?"

"November something, before the baby was born." She looked at her sandwich. "We'll have to buy Lorrie some groceries to replace these."

"What else did you find for 1842?"

"A big black book of slaves bought and sold," she said, her lip curling. "I couldn't look at it. That's one aspect of American history I can't abide. Human beings put on an auction block and–"

Nick put his hand on her arm. "At least the publication of the records can help people find their ancestors."

"True," she said. "Maybe afterward I can find–"

"What's that sound?"

Holly listened for a second, then jumped up. "It's my cell phone." Her bag was on the floor by the front door. She ran to the hall, grabbed her phone and listened, her face falling with every second. She said good-bye then went back to the kitchen.

"That was Taylor. I have a fitting today. She says she told me about it, but I didn't remember."

She looked so forlorn that Nick put his arm around her shoulders. "Your dad said I had to look after you only while you were here. How about if you drop me off at Spring Hill, I get my truck, you go to your fitting, and I'll go to the local library? If Jason Beaumont was hanged the newspapers will be full of it."

"Can you? I mean, do you–?"

He pulled away from her, one eyebrow raised. "Do I know how to research? Sure. It's easy." He stepped back, unbuttoned his shirt halfway down, gave her a lascivious look, and said, "So what do you have on Belle Chere in 1842?" He looked like a very sexy gang member.

Holly laughed. "You're incorrigible."

"If it works it'll be worth it. Remember, I want the job."

"Job?" she said and felt guilty, as though he'd read her mind about her idea of sending him off to Hollander Tools. "Oh, you mean as manager of Belle Chere after I . . . after I . . ."

"After you marry the owner of this place."

"Yeah," she said, but was unable to meet his eyes.

Nick put his hand under her chin and lifted her eyes to meet his. "Come on, now, you're not falling in love with me, are you?"

"Not even close. I was thinking that you cannot possibly work here after Lorrie and I–I mean, if Lorrie and I–" She glared at him. "You nearly went crazy last night when Lorrie kissed me." She expected Nick to deny it, but he didn't.

"You ready to go?" he asked, no humor in his voice. "This research might take a while."

Holly got up from her chair and followed Nick outside to the car. Again, she thought how Nick was the only difficulty in her plans for the future. If she could just take Nick out of the picture, she felt sure that everything would work out the way she wanted it to.

She glanced at him as he started the car and thought that the problem was that she didn't want Nick to leave. She needed his help on the research and she needed– Truthfully, there wasn't anything she actually needed him for. Except maybe sex. Fabulous sex. Earth shaking sex. The best sex–

"Keep looking at me like that and you'll never make your appointment."

She glanced to her right. Through the trees she could see Belle Chere. It was absurd to love a house so much, but what she really loved was a way of life. She could see herself in that house with three children. She saw herself in meetings with local and national preservationists.

She turned to look at Nick. What she couldn't see was herself living with him. Nick joked and teased, but she could see that he was a proud man. He wouldn't want to live off his wife–which meant that Holly would have to try to live on *his* earnings.

Holly looked away. I'm a snob, she thought. And lazy. I don't want to spend my days doing the laundry. I want–

For a moment, she closed her eyes. It was better to think about her dissertation than to try to predetermine her future.

# Chapter Eleven

"Darci?" Nick said into the phone. "Are you busy?"

"Never too busy for you. How is everyone?"

"Fine. Great," he said impatiently. Darci Montgomery was his cousin's wife and she was clairvoyant.

"What's wrong?" she asked.

"You tell me," Nick said and gave a nervous laugh.

"Okay. There's a woman near you and there's a big hole full of gold."

"It does exist then?" he asked. "I wasn't sure. There's a man here who says a treasure was buried by his relative over a hundred years ago, but he's not somebody I like. He–"

"It's possible that he's going to marry the woman you love."

"I do not love her!" Nick said indignantly.

"That's like saying an acorn isn't an oak tree."

"Huh?"

"Acorns grow; love grows. Your love for her now is the size of an acorn, but it'll soon be the size of an oak."

"Great news, since you just said she's probably going to marry someone else," Nick said.

"One thing about the future is that it can be changed. Nick," Darci said, "there's something wrong there. I'm not sure what it is, but something is wrong. It's as though I'm seeing two visions at the same time. This young woman has dark hair?"

"Yeah," Nick said softly. "And a body like out of an under-wear catalog. Today she had on–"

Darci's laugh cut him off. "There are some scenes I don't need to see."

"So we find this treasure, then she marries the guy with the big house," Nick said gloomily.

Darci was quiet for a moment. "What are you up to? You can afford to buy the biggest house in America–and so can she. You know that, don't you?"

"Yeah. Hollander Tools. I can't go into the details now, but she thinks I'm poor, uneducated, and . . . You get the idea."

"I guess that's why I see lies all around you. If you tell her who you are she'll tell you she loves you."

"Does she?" he asked eagerly.

"All I see is confusion around her. I feel sorry for her. She likes you a lot, but she *loves* her family. In her mind, if she loves you she'll lose her family. It's not fair that you're trying to make her choose between you and her family."

"Yeah, I know," Nick said. "I'm a genuine cad."

Darci laughed. "Definitely! But, Nick, listen, there's some real danger around you. Someone's watching you both."

"For the treasure or for Holly's inheritance?"

"Both. There's something there that needs feeding and it eats gold. Does that make sense?"

"Oh, yeah. It's a big house complete with outbuildings. It looks like a set from *Gone With the Wind*. It's what Holly *truly* loves."

"No. She truly loves her family. Nick—"

"So what about this guy Lorrie? The guy you say she's going to marry?"

"Danger to him or from him, I don't know which."

"Not from him, but there's danger he may walk into my fist if he doesn't keep his hands off Holly. So, tell me, any ideas where this treasure is?"

"It's in a big hole in the ground, a natural cave, but a small one. There's a tree growing over the opening. The two men who put the gold in the ground planted the tree and now you can't see the hole. The only way you'll find it is— You know, I'm not going to tell you that. If you dig through the old records and use your brains, you and your girlfriend will be able to find it. But, you know something, that man, Lorrie?"

"Yes?"

"He doesn't believe it exists. He just wants Holly there. Nick, please tell her who you are."

"I'll think about it," he said, wanting to change the subject. He didn't want Darci telling him what he already knew, that he was doing a low-down, despicable thing to a very nice person. "So what have you been up to lately?"

"Oh, the usual, setting ghosts free, collecting magic objects, hauling dead men back from the light. Same ol', same ol'."

Nick laughed. "I miss you. Any word on . . . ?"

He heard Darci swallow. "Adam and Bo? No, no word, but I think I may be closer. The FBI– Oh well, my story can wait. Why don't you send me some things owned by the people you've been telling me about and let me see what I can feel? I've got this 'Touch of God' now and–"

"A what?"

"It's too long to go into. I'll tell you later. I know I can use it to help raise the dead, but I'm not sure what else I can do with it."

"And here I've been excited about some silly ol' treasure. Raising the dead, huh?"

"Only one dead man and I had a lot of help."

"Oh. That's a disappointment. I was hoping you'd done it all alone."

Darci laughed. "I miss you, too. Send me the things and– I have to go. Linc's here."

"Linc who?" Nick asked sharply.

"Don't worry, there's no other man in my life. It's Lincoln Aimes."

"The actor?" Nick's voice rose.

"Want an autographed picture?"

"No, I . . ."

Darci laughed again. "You want to be reassured that I still love my husband, your cousin. Oh, yes. More than ever. Forever. Now I have to go. Linc and I and the girls are going out."

"How's your father?" Nick asked before she hung up.

"He's in Mesopotamia."

"Does it still exist?"

"It does in Georgia. He's talking to a blind man who isn't really blind. I have to go! Good-bye, Nick, and tell her who and what you are. You're torturing her."

Smiling, Nick hung up. "Torturing, huh?" he said aloud and liked the sound of it. Holly in her teeny-tiny white underwear, standing in front of a fan, leaning over boxes, had nearly sent him into an insane asylum. "Turnabout's fair play," he said, then tossed the truck keys in the air and caught them. He had some research to do.

# Chapter Twelve

The fitting for the bridesmaid dress was worse than Holly had imagined. The dress was awful: lavender chiffon, off one shoulder, with a wrapping of foot-wide ruffles. The double ruffle started at one shoulder, spiraled down under her arm, across her back, across her hip, then down over her thighs. When she took a step, the wide ruffling floated out around her so that she felt as though she were wearing Frisbees.

"Taylor!" she said, sending a pleading glance to her stepsister in the mirror. Of course, Holly didn't plan to wear the awful dress, and instead planned to wear a bridal gown, but still . . .

"Don't worry about it. You look great. Just think about what you're going to make *me* wear at *your* wedding."

"Does that mean you know something I don't?"

"With the way Lorrie was looking at you last night, I think you'll be in white within a year."

"You think so?" Holly said, still looking at Taylor in the

mirror. Absently, she held the necklace Nick had given her.

"What is that?"

"Nothing," Holly said and dropped the necklace back into her bra.

"It's from a man, isn't it? Wait! Don't tell me. It's from the two-days-of-divine-sex guy, isn't it?"

"Yeah," Holly said slowly, her face turning red.

"So let's see it."

Holly turned away. "It's just a cheap necklace. I'm sure my neck's going to turn green from the chain." She put her hand over the top of her dress protectively.

"Hmmm," Taylor said. "Should I tell Lorrie he has competition?"

"Of course not!" Holly snapped, then looked at Taylor in conspiracy. "Well, maybe a little competition. Just to spice things up."

"Speaking of spice, how was your day out with the lawnmower boy?"

"Nick? He dozed in a hammock while I nearly died of the heat in the attic." She turned away so her sister wouldn't see her face.

"Hammock, huh? Maybe I should go with you tomorrow."

"You do and I'll put you to work. There are thousands upon thousands of ledgers and letters to go through."

Taylor shivered. "No, thank you. So what are you planning for the weekend?"

"Nothing much. Research, I guess."

"Will Lorrie be back?"

"I have no idea," Holly said, frowning. Taylor's teasing made her see that she'd had little contact with Lorrie. He hadn't made a date with her or even arranged to see her again.

Taylor smiled. "Come on, don't look so glum. He kissed you in front of our parents, didn't he? And he gave you a key to his house. If he did any more it would have involved a clergyman."

"Yeah, I guess so," Holly said, but she was hesitant.

"Cheer up," Taylor said, looking at her watch. "I have to go. Charles is waiting for me."

"As he has been for years."

"Yeah," Taylor said, grinning. "You get out of that dress and take some time off. Go shopping."

"Sure," Holly said as she slipped into the dressing room. As soon as she was in decent clothes again, she planned to go to the library. Maybe Nick would still be there.

For a moment she looked at herself in the dressing room mirror. She had on white underwear, lacy and nice, but not exactly set-a-man-on-fire. Between her breasts lay the necklace Nick had given her. What had he said? He liked the display case.

Maybe instead of going to the library she'd go shopping. About fifty miles away was a huge shopping center. Maybe she'd see about buying some new underwear. For Lorrie, she told herself. For Lorrie.

Once on the street, Taylor snapped open her cell phone and dialed a number from the memory. It was answered on the second ring.

"If you want her, you'd better get down here," Taylor said, then waited. "I really couldn't care less about what I'm sure is your very interesting and unique sex life. Something is going on with her and I don't like it." She paused. "If I knew what it was, I'd fix it. I think it has to do with that guy who cuts the grass." Pause. "No, she's not having sex with him. She's a prude. She– Good Lord! You might be right. Maybe he's the one she–" Taylor cut herself off. "If you want to save that rotting old house of yours, I suggest that you get down here now!" She snapped the phone closed, then smiled at the memory of her stepsister in that awful bridesmaid dress. Dear, sweet, lovable, *rich* Holly, she thought. Holly, who everyone loved, who everyone adored. Holly, who had been given everything all her life.

Still smiling, Taylor looked through the restaurant window at her fiancé Charles and waved. How much do I hate thee? she thought. Let me count the ways. Smiling more broadly, she went inside.

# Chapter Thirteen

It was after dinner and Holly was in her bedroom. Her parents were in the sitting room downstairs, watching a movie on the TV, and Taylor was in her room talking on the phone to someone.

Holly was cutting the price tags off her many new sets of underwear while watching the driveway for lights from Nick's truck. It was already after nine, so where had he been all afternoon? She knew he wasn't driving that monster truck he'd had in the garage when she'd met him, but was his beat-up old truck secretly a racer? Had he met with other truck-racing people and started placing bets? Was he now in the backseat with some girl with four feet of black hair and hoop earrings six inches in diameter?

She told herself to get a grip. She had no right to be jealous. No right—

She broke off because she saw Nick's headlights coming down the long drive. Hastily, she shoved her new underwear into the shopping bag and pushed it under her bed. It wasn't that she wanted to hide anything, but if Taylor saw, she'd tease Holly a lot.

Quietly, Holly tiptoed down the stairs, grateful to the people who'd restored the house that the steps didn't creak. She slipped out the kitchen door, down the stairs, and across the lawn to the tiny house where Nick was living. By rights the house should have been given to Roger and Phyllis, the couple who'd taken care of her parents for over twenty years. But a year ago, after James Latham had called Roger at 3:00 A.M. four nights in a row, they made new rules, one of which was that they would live off-site.

She saw the back of Nick disappear into the little house, a grocery bag in each arm. She went to the truck, hauled out two more bags, and went to the house. She met Nick on his way out again. She saw his surprise, then his look of pleasure, then the way he tried to look emotionless.

"Out for a walk?" he asked.

She held the back door open for him. "Out to find out if you discovered anything."

"Maybe," he said, setting the groceries on the counter. He began to put them away.

The kitchen was tiny and there wasn't room for two of them, so Holly sat on the countertop. Shamelessly, she stretched her bare legs, exposed by her short shorts, across the doorway to the other counter.

"Like maybe what?" she asked, picking up a package of rice and pretending to read the label.

Nick took the package out of her hand and put it in the cabinet. "So what's this all about?" he asked, nodding toward her bare legs. "You want me to scratch your itch while your boyfriend's out of town?"

Holly started to pull her legs up, but made herself stay where she was. "So what's put you in a bad mood? Get a librarian who wasn't interested? Or did you make a pass at some motorcycle chick and she turned you down?"

"None of the above. Could you move?"

Holly hesitated, but Nick was frowning so deeply she pulled her legs up to let him pass. "What's wrong with you?" she asked as he left the kitchen.

"I've been wrestling with my conscience," he said over his shoulder as he went down the hall to where there was a bedroom and bath.

Holly got off the counter, went into the little living room, and looked about. It was as she remembered the building, nothing interesting or special about it. Marguerite had furnished it prettily, with a sofa and chairs and a few knick-knacks that wouldn't fit into the main house.

But there wasn't one item in the room that was personal to Nick. There were no photographs, no souvenirs, no books, not even any magazines.

Nick came into the room, slipping a T-shirt over his head.

"So what do you want?" Turning, he went back to the kitchen.

What was wrong with him? She stood in the kitchen door and watched as he opened the refrigerator door and looked inside. She went to him, put her hands on his shoulders, and pushed him to sit down at the little two-seat table in front of the window. "You talk and I'll make you a six-egg omelet. Deal?"

"Yeah, okay," he said with a grudging smile. He took a beer out of the 'fridge, opened it, then sat down at the table and watched her as he started talking. "The story wasn't exactly as you told me. First of all, Jason's trial and hanging were in a town a hundred miles from here."

"A hundred miles?!" She broke eggs into a bowl and began to mince onions and green pepper.

"As far as I could tell, Arthur was worse than we thought. An early newspaper account said that Arthur had begged to have the trial moved to another town so Jason would be sure to receive justice."

"Because people in Edenton knew the victims?"

"That's what was reported, but one newspaper said the victim was 'notorious' for his dishonest scales. Half the men in town had threatened to kill him and his wife since she worked with him."

Holly stopped chopping and looked at Nick. "If that's so, then it makes no sense to move the trial. The defense attorney could have put lots of people on the stand to swear that they, too, had threatened the victim."

Nick sipped his beer. "Wait. This gets better."

"You like mushrooms?"

"Sure. The newspapers reported that Jason was very relaxed during the trial. In fact, one time he fell asleep and the judge bawled him out."

"He wasn't worried about four witnesses against him?"

"Apparently not, but then his three lawyers—"

"Three!"

"Yeah, three attorneys and two assistants. They made mincemeat of the witnesses. It was dark, they'd been drinking, and their characters weren't of the best. This was before a person's past criminal record was inadmissable in court, so every crime those four had been involved in was told to the jury."

Holly mixed the eggs and dumped them into a hot skillet lavished with butter. "So that left Arthur's testimony to get his brother off."

When Nick didn't answer, she looked at him, saw that he was frowning. "What's upset you?" she asked.

"I believe in family loyalty. It's something my family thinks highly of. We've always believed—" He took a breath and looked at her. "Jason could sleep in the courtroom because he knew his brother would get him off by telling the truth. But when Arthur got on the stand he started crying and said he couldn't lie, that Jason had not been with him that night."

"And the lawyers couldn't discredit him," Holly said, sliding the fat, juicy omelet onto a plate and putting it in front of Nick.

"Right. Hey! This is good. Arthur had been very careful to show no jealousy when Julia broke their engagement to marry his younger brother. In fact, Arthur had told half a dozen people that his brother had done him a favor. He hinted that he'd been planning to break the engagement anyway and that Jason had taken 'used goods' off his hands."

"'Used goods,' " Holly said, sneering. "What a horrible concept. No one saw it as sour grapes?"

"I guess not. Arthur had been too good an actor; he fooled everyone."

Holly finished cleaning the skillet and sat down across from Nick. "So Arthur cried on the stand and sent his innocent brother to the gallows."

"Exactly."

Absently, Holly picked up Nick's bottle of beer and drank from it. "What about when Jason married Julia? That happened three days before he was hanged. Was he actually allowed out of jail or was he allowed to marry her while he was in jail because she was pregnant?" She looked at him. "Do you think Jason really took all of Belle Chere's movable wealth and buried it? Or is that a myth?"

Nick drained the beer and got up to get another bottle. "It's true. Big hole with a tree planted over it." As soon as he said it, his eyes widened and he put the beer to his lips.

Holly picked up his fork and took a bite of his omelet. "Tree, huh?"

"At least that's my fantasy," he said as he grinned much too wide.

"A big hole with a tree planted over it. Your very own . . . ? What did you call it? A fantasy?"

"Yeah," Nick said, eyes on his plate, his mouth full.

"Golly. Most men I know fantasize about silk underwear."

"Yeah," he said, looking at her with hot eyes. "A white bra and panties and a great big fan."

When he reached out his hand to take hers, she leaned back in her chair. "But you fantasize about big holes full of gold with a tree growing over it. So who planted the tree?"

"How would I know? I didn't get that far in my fantasy. Who do *you* think planted the tree?"

She narrowed her eyes at him. "So help me, Nick Taggert, if you don't tell me what you know I'll go crying to my father and tell him I had sex with you and you broke my heart."

"Blackmail?" His eyes were twinkling.

"The blackest."

He pushed his empty plate away and leaned back in his chair. "It's not that I don't want to tell you, it's just that you won't believe me."

"Why not? Disreputable source?"

"Not really. I mean, she's very reputable, it's just that . . ."

"What?" Holly asked, looking hard at him and racking her brain to figure out what he was being so hesitant about. She watched him open his mouth four times, but no words came out. If the treasure hadn't been buried in 1842, she'd have thought that he was hiding the fact that he got the news from a criminal. From some pal of one of the participants. Maybe a cousin of his who was "doin' time" for armed robbery.

Nick kept nursing his beer, then seemed to become interested in the darkness outside the window.

Who? she thought. What? "A clairvoyant," Holly said at last, smiling at her own cleverness. "Did she look into a crystal ball or did you call someone over the Internet?"

When Nick looked at her in anger, she frowned. He was certainly in a bad mood tonight. He got out of his chair and held the door open for her. "Good night, Miss Latham," he said formally.

Holly didn't move and stayed in her chair. "You want to tell me what's wrong with you?" she said.

"Why? So you can share it with the man you plan to marry?"

"No," she said slowly, "because we're friends. We can be friends, can't we?"

Nick took a while before he answered, while still holding the back door open. "The woman who told me this information is a clairvoyant, but she's not a charlatan. She doesn't take clients in person or over the Internet. In private, with no praise, and no reward, she helps the government find criminals, especially child molesters. She's a relative of mine by marriage and I'll hear no disparaging word against her."

"Okay," Holly said softly, looking at him. He really did take family loyalty seriously!

Nick closed the door, got two beers out of the refrigerator, handed her one, then went into the living room, Holly following him. She sat on the couch and he took a chair across from her.

"You okay?" she asked after a while.

"Yeah. Too soft a heart, I guess. Brother against brother. I hate that."

"Have any of your brothers betrayed you?"

"You want to quit treating me like I'm a nut case?"

"Actually, I was thinking that if you don't tell me soon what the clairvoyant said I'll throw this bottle of beer at you."

Nick smiled, drank deeply of his beer, and smiled more. "That's better."

"You're not an alcoholic, are you?"

"Nymphomaniac," he said seriously. "It's a real problem with me." He looked at her with lazy, sexy eyes.

She picked up a pillow and threw it at him, but he caught it. "Tell me!" she demanded.

"The treasure is in a small cave with a hole in the top. The two men who stole it put it in there, then covered the hole and planted a tree over it. The tree's big now so you can't see the hole."

"And?"

"And if we search through the records and use our brains we'll be able to find it."

"What else?"

"That's it. We *can* find the treasure."

Holly blinked at him. "Did you get a date on that discovery? How long before we find it? How much research do we have to do? If I have to read all the papers in the attic I'll be a hundred years old before—"

"Before you can present it to Lorrie and claim the prize of becoming Mrs. Belle Chere?"

Suddenly, she was sick of his bad mood. "What should I do? Marry *you* instead? Maybe we could live here, in this house. Maybe my father would give this house to us as a wedding present."

"At least it would be better than selling your soul for a house!"

"You make me sick," she said, standing up.

He stood up. "You don't exactly make me feel great. What twenty-first-century woman connives as you have to get a man to the altar? You're throwing yourself at me, parading around in your tiny underwear, but you're trying to *buy* him."

"That's disgusting! I'm doing no such thing. I was on my way here to see Lorrie when I met you."

"Yeah and what did you do? Attacked me in the backseat of the car, that's what."

She stepped close to him, looking him in the eye. "I was grateful and stupid. I should have known that a man like you wouldn't know the meaning of the word 'honor.' "

"And this Lorrie does? Today I read of a trial in which one of your Lorrie's ancestors sent his own brother to be hanged. All for that house you're selling yourself for. You're a fitting match for the Beaumonts."

"Why you—"

Holly drew back her hand to strike him, but Nick caught her wrist. For a moment they stood there, breathing hard in anger, then the next moment their mouths were together and they fell onto the couch.

Shirts, buttons, shorts, trousers, all came off in seconds. To Holly it seemed as though it had been years since she'd felt Nick's hands on her body. Today, in that stifling attic, with sweat dripping off her, she'd wanted him, wanted to feel his damp, hot body against hers, but, as he'd promised, he'd stayed away from her.

Now the desire of the morning, and the wait of the evening, fueled her passion until her fingertips were digging into his skin and pulling him closer and closer.

Her left leg was flung over the back of the couch, and her right knee was bent as Nick entered her hard. She moaned and his mouth overtook hers.

Their passion had built throughout the day until they were desperate for each other. When the top half of Holly slid off the couch, Nick went with her until they were making love on the floor, pounding, desperate, hot love.

When they came, Holly arched her hips and Nick held her to him.

For a moment they stayed together, shuddering in the aftershock of their passion.

Nick rolled off of her, then pulled her head onto his shoulder. "Feel better?" he asked and she nodded against him. "Me, too. You wouldn't want to move to the bedroom, would you?"

"I can't," she said. "My father—"

He kissed her to silence. "Tomorrow's my day off. How about if I rent a boat and we go—"

"Treasure hunting?" Holly asked.

"I was thinking we could go fishing."

"Belle Chere has—"

"No Belle Chere, no Beaumonts, no Jason or Arthur. Just a boat and some fishing poles." When she didn't answer he said, "Okay, you win. Picnic on the dock at Belle Chere and I'll haul down six of those trunks full of papers for you."

"Oh, Nick, would you?" She sat up on one elbow and looked at him. "That really would be wonderful. You could fish and I could read." She kissed him to thank him, but he put his hand on the back of her head and deepened the kiss.

After a moment she pulled away and saw the clock on the top of the bookcase. "It's nearly eleven! I have to go. If my father . . ." She waved her hand to indicate she had no idea what he'd do if he found out she was gone.

"And you're how old?"

"To him, I'm about eight."

Hastily, Holly dressed, then stood and looked at Nick, still lying on the floor, completely nude. For a moment she fought the urge to throw off her clothes and lie down beside him. She'd like to spend the night with him. She'd like to lie in his arms and snuggle all night.

"I have to go," she said quickly before she changed her mind, then she turned on her heel and ran out of the house. Minutes later she quietly opened the kitchen door of the big house—and nearly ran into Taylor.

"Where have you been?" Taylor hissed, but didn't give Holly a chance to answer. "You look horrible. Go to the powder room and do what you can with yourself."

"But it's late and—"

"Lorrie is sitting in the living room. He wants to see you. He came back from his trip early just to see *you*. Now go on, do something with yourself."

Holly scurried into the powder room.

# Chapter Fourteen

"YOU LOOK BEAUTIFUL," LORRIE SAID, SMILING at her.

They were in an old-fashioned wooden canoe, Lorrie rowing them slowly down the river leading to Belle Chere. Taylor had supervised Holly's dressing that morning so she was wearing a narrow cotton-lace skirt that kept wrapping around her legs. Twice Lorrie had had to catch her before she fell.

Last night when he'd invited her out for today, she hadn't been able to say that she had a previous engagement with the gardener, so she'd accepted.

The next day, Taylor took so much time in dressing Holly she'd not been able to slip out to tell Nick in person that she wouldn't see him that day. Instead, she'd seen him in the kitchen, talking to her father, and she'd loudly reiterated her plans for the day. Nick had listened but made no comment.

"Now try on this blouse. Lorrie will love it."

Holly wasn't sure how Taylor thought she knew what Lorrie would like, but she allowed herself to be dressed in linen and lace, all of it white and easily dirtied. There'd be no hiking in the swamp looking for tree-covered cave entrances.

Promptly at ten, Lorrie had picked her up, and immediately, Holly had started questioning him about Arthur and Jason and Julia.

Lorrie laughed in a pleasant way. "I seem to have unleashed a flood. Holly dearest, I know no more than I told you. I'm afraid that over the years that story has become merely a dinner party entertainment. Told only to a select few, of course."

"Oh," Holly said, disappointed, then told herself to grow up. Not everyone was fascinated with history, even if it involved injustice and a lost treasure. She made herself relax against the leather of Lorrie's BMW and told herself she had to make conversation. Since she was usually with other preservationists and academics, it was a long time since she'd had a simple chat. On the other hand, she never seemed to have trouble talking to Nick. But what did they talk about? The word "sex" came to her mind.

At that thought her face turned red and she looked out the side window. When Lorrie took her hand, she looked back.

"A penny . . ." he said.

"I was just thinking that it had been a long time since I'd talked about anything except work."

"Me, either," he said. "Shall we ban talk of work for the day? Yours and mine." He gave her a sideways look. "And Belle Chere."

Holly wrinkled her brow. "No work? No Belle Chere? What else is there?"

They laughed together, then Lorrie spoke. "Tell me every word of everything you've done since you were thirteen."

"Okay, so there's fifteen minutes of the day gone, then what?"

"That I don't believe. A beautiful woman like you?" He lifted her hand and kissed the palm. "You must have had a million proposals of marriage by now."

She started to say she hadn't, but changed her mind. "Only eight hundred and twelve thousand, give or take one or two."

"No more? Surely . . . ?"

Again, they laughed together. Holly leaned back in the seat and smiled. This is going to work out well, she thought.

However, two hours later, she was bored. It was one thing to see romantic photos of a lady in white being rowed down the river by a handsome man, but quite another to experience it. The truth was, she'd like to take off her clothes and go skinny-dipping.

But not with Lorrie. With Nick.

She took a deep breath and told herself to stop that. "So tell me about your marriage." That question should liven things up!

"What do you think about air-conditioning Belle Chere?" Lorrie asked, his eyes laughing.

"Oh! So I'm to confess all, but you're to tell me nothing?"

"Might I point out that you've told me nothing whatever about yourself."

"What should I tell you? That the summer I spent with you at Belle Chere changed my life?"

"That's a good start. Go on."

Briefly, she told him how she'd kept the love of old houses that he'd instilled in her, and that all she needed now was to complete her Ph.D. She trailed her hand in the water. "And since you asked me to help you find the treasure . . ."

When Lorrie grunted, she looked at him. "My darling Hollander," he said softly, "I fear that that treasure is a myth. Truthfully, I had completely dishonorable intentions in telling that story."

"But Nick said it was real," she blurted, then closed her mouth firmly.

"And who is Nick?"

Looking away, Holly said, "He works for us."

"The gardener?" Lorrie asked in disbelief. "You're quoting the *gardener?*"

"He's a nice guy," Holly said defensively.

"I'm sure he is. However, I can't see how he'd have any insight into my family's history." Lorrie chuckled. "Unless he's psychic, of course."

Again, Holly looked away, her face even redder, and she thought how silly it had been for her to believe Nick. A clairvoyant! she thought. A cave with a tree planted over it. How absurd. "I really would like to know about your marriage," she said to distract Lorrie.

As he rowed, he began to tell her of his former marriage. As far as Holly could tell, Lorrie had married the older woman out of pity. Her husband had always taken care of her and after the man died, as her lawyer, Lorrie had had to spend masses of time with her as he sorted through her husband's many businesses.

"She was lonely," Lorrie said, "and for the first time since she was nineteen she had no man to take care of her. When she was going to cancel attending a charity ball because she had no escort, I volunteered to go with her. After that, one thing led to another, and . . ." He looked at Holly with sad eyes. "I'm ashamed to say that I was dazzled by her. She was a very beautiful and very wealthy woman. There were yacht parties and summer cottages with a dozen bedrooms. Being with her was like living in a past time. A time"—he lowered his voice—"such as when Belle Chere was at its peak. She made me feel like my ancestors must have felt when they gave parties for three hundred people."

He stopped rowing. "Can you forgive me?"

"Forgive you?" she asked. "For what?"

"For being too young and foolish to have seen what was right under my nose when I first met you."

"I forgive you," she said. "And I was just a kid that summer."

"Yeah, and I'd sworn off women for the entire summer."

She'd always wanted to hear his side of why he'd given up a social life with kids his own age. "So tell me everything," she said, and he talked some more.

By four o'clock, Holly felt much better than she had earlier. All in all, she and Lorrie had had a lovely day. He was a wonderful raconteur, and he'd told story after story about his family, past and present, and about his law practice. There were a couple of times when she thought he was being a bit indiscreet, but his confidences only made her feel as though he trusted her—and that he planned to keep her in his future life.

By 4:30, they were at Belle Chere and all the lethargy of the day fell away as they walked through the gardens and inspected every inch of the plantation. In daylight, Holly saw much more deterioration than she'd seen at night. Roofs were in bad shape; walls sagged. Rats were gnawing at floorboards. Owls were nesting. And the weeds! Vines grew up through floors and out windows.

Holly said little but she saw a lot. At this rate, in about fifteen years, Belle Chere would be in ruins. All that would be left would be piles of rotting wood. People would say, "There used to a cotton gin over there."

It was all she could do not to beg Lorrie to allow her to pay for restoring the place, but he'd told her that when he and his wealthy wife had divorced his pride had allowed him to take nothing from her. She was sure that a man of such pride would never allow someone else to pay his expenses. In fact, he said he'd used all his savings to prevent his former wife from taking Belle Chere in the property settlement.

"But how could she have taken it?" Holly asked, shocked. "It was yours before you married."

"Her attorneys said that she'd paid millions to renovate Belle Chere so it belonged to her as much as to me. I didn't delve into what falsehoods she'd told her accountants."

"Didn't anyone come out here to look at this place?" She twirled around. "There's been no money put into Belle Chere for many years. It's falling down."

"That bad, huh?" Lorrie was smiling at her.

Holly stopped twirling and looked at her hands. "It does need some work." Maybe it was because they'd met when she was still a child, but sometimes Lorrie seemed very old to her. Which, of course, was ridiculous. The truth was, he was only twenty-seven. And Nick had told her he was twenty-nine. But it was Lorrie who seemed old. No, she corrected herself, Lorrie seemed mature. Sophisticated. He'd been through a lot in his short life and it showed in his eyes and manners.

Reaching out his hand, he caressed her cheek. "You have a way of looking at me that makes me feel as though I could lasso the moon."

She kept her eyes down, but she was pleased by his words. When he took a step closer to her, she held her breath.

"I don't think I realized how much a pair of velvet eyes have haunted me all these years. It's true that that summer you were a kid and I was nursing a broken heart over . . ." Pausing, he chuckled. "Over a fellow student, so all I wanted to do was work and forget. But, later, I thought about you often."

He put his hand under her chin and lifted her eyes to look at him. "Did you ever think about me in all those years? Not as the owner of all this, but as a man?"

"Now and then," she said, trying not to bat her lashes too hard, but he was making her feel very coquettish.

"If I hadn't been so distracted that summer . . ." He bent his head as he leaned down, his lips moving close to hers.

But he didn't kiss her because suddenly the sound of a motorcycle made them both look up.

Nick, wearing a dark helmet, sunglasses, T-shirt, jeans, and tall black boots, came roaring toward them on an enormous motorcycle that looked as though it had served in a couple of wars.

He skidded to a stop so close to them that Holly jumped back, but Lorrie held his ground, refusing to move an inch. Lorrie had an odd expression on his face that Holly couldn't read.

Nick yelled at Holly over the blare of the big machine, but she could only make out the words "father" and "home."

"What?!" she yelled back at him.

"Your father–" Nick shouted then turned the accelerator so the giant motorcycle emitted more noise and a lot of smoke. "Home!" Nick finished.

Lorrie reached out and killed the motor of the bike and the resulting silence was thunderous.

"Why'd you do that?" Nick asked. "It takes forever to get this thing started again." He looked at Holly. "Your father wants you home *now*."

"Is something wrong?" Her hand went to her throat. Since her father's heart attack, she'd worried about him every minute.

Nick shrugged. "I'm just the gardener. He told me he needed you now so here I am. But the last time I saw him he looked and sounded healthy."

"I will take Miss Latham home," Lorrie said, still looking quite strange.

"In that?" Nick asked, nodding toward Lorrie's BMW. "It has a flat. Probably a nail in the tire. Holly better go back with me. If I can get this thing started again, that is."

She looked at Lorrie. "I'd better go with him," she said, putting on the passenger helmet. "My father may need me."

"Of course," Lorrie said graciously as he put his hands on her shoulders.

She knew he meant to kiss her on the lips as he'd done the last time he'd been confronted by Nick, but she turned away.

For one thing, she'd bent toward him three times that day, making it easy for him to kiss her, but he hadn't. In the second place, since she planned to get on a motorcycle that Nick was driving, she didn't want him angry.

"I'll see you . . . tomorrow?" she asked Lorrie as she backed away from him.

"Yes, please do stop by," he said stiffly.

"No, I mean in the morning. For research. For my doctorate."

"Ah, yes, of course," Lorrie said, then smiled. "Yes, do come early. For breakfast. And since I'll be here you won't need a chaperone." He looked pointedly at Nick. "We can–" He said no more as Nick kick-started the big motorcycle and drowned out all conversation.

Shrugging, Holly stepped toward the bike, but the long skirt she was wearing prevented her from straddling the back. In the next second, Lorrie picked her up by the waist and sat her sidesaddle on the back of the motorcycle, her skirt hiked up uncomfortably.

Lorrie stepped back, kissed his fingertips, and blew her a kiss. Holly knew Nick was watching so she returned the gesture–then had to grab Nick when he sent the bike flying down the driveway.

She wasn't in the least surprised when he went past Spring Hill's driveway and headed toward Edenton. Surprised, no, but angry, yes. He was assuming too much! She yelled into his ear that she wanted him to stop.

He pulled off the road and into the parking lot of a closed antiques shop, and parked in the shade. "You want to tell me what that was all about?" she demanded as she got off the bike and removed the helmet.

He took off his helmet and ran his hand through his sweaty hair.

"Would you please answer me?" she snapped. "And how dare you use my father's name in a lie!"

"We're friends, remember?" Nick said, unperturbed. "So how do you like my new bike?"

"New? That thing was probably used in a Marlon Brando movie."

"Yeah," he said, grinning. "That's what I thought, too. Maybe I should buy a leather jacket and one of those flat-topped motorcycle caps. How do you think I'd look?"

She glared at him.

"Okay, okay, keep your shirt on. On the other hand . . ."

Holly glared at him harder.

"Two things. You spent too much time with him on the first date."

"Are you crazy?! I *slept* with *you* on the first date."

"Actually, I'm not sure you'd classify any of our time to-gether as a 'date.' And since you're not planning to marry me it doesn't matter what you do with me. But ol' Lorrie—"

"He's two years younger than you are."

"But he seems older, don't you think? Or maybe it's the button-down shirt and the creased slacks and the penny loafers. Didn't they go out of style in about 1952? Speaking of clothes, what do you have on? Under that, I mean?" He reached toward her.

When she took a step back, he stopped. "Sorry," he murmured.

"Could we start again?" she asked. "Why did you pick me up at Lorrie's? And did you give his car a flat?"

He removed a blue bandanna from his back pocket and began to polish the chrome gas tank—which was useless since the chrome was pitted with corrosion. When he spoke, his voice was no longer joking. "Yesterday you said we were friends so I was trying to help you. Guys like Lorrie—"

"Please refrain from stereotyping him," she said stiffly.

"Okay, sorry again." He pushed the bandanna back into his pocket, then leaned against the motorcycle, his arms folded across his chest. "I can see you won't believe me, but I *was* trying to help you. You need to play a little bit hard to get. No man appreciates what comes too easily. It's the caveman thing. We like the hunt."

"So I guess since I came to you, that makes me—"

"You! You're kidding, aren't you? You're not just hard to get, you're impossible. Oh, sure, I can have your body anytime I want it. All I have to do is—" When she gave him a warning look, he stopped. "Okay, so that's not the point. *I* am not the point. The point is that friends, just as you said we are, help each other. Isn't that a song?"

"Nick, so help me, if you—"

"Okay, as I was saying, you can't go on a first date with a guy and spend—what was it? six hours with him. You need to make him want more. In six hours you probably told him everything about yourself, including how you've dreamed about his house for eleven years."

"Him, not Belle Chere. I dreamed about *him*. The house is a bonus."

"I see. Like Lorrie's the job and the paycheck is the bonus. One's good and one's bad."

She narrowed her eyes at him.

"Okay, sorry yet again, but can you blame me? I lost and he won. Not because he's a better man than I am, but because he. . . . Tell me again why he's winning and I'm not."

Holly stepped toward the motorcycle, ready to demand that Nick return her to Spring Hill.

"Before I showed up today, had he said anything about date number two? Before *you* asked *him* out, that is?"

Holly didn't answer, but she halted and turned back to look at him.

"So let me ask you this," Nick continued. "Today, what did you two talk about? Your life or his?"

She didn't want to answer that question because they'd talked almost totally about Lorrie's life. Of course, Holly had insisted that they do so. Every time her life had come up, she'd been the one to change the subject. However, Nick's words made her think. He had always drawn her out. As he'd said, he was a good listener.

"You're a wicked man, Nick Taggert."

"No, I'm a man who likes you. In fact, I like you too much, so I'm going to try to keep you from making mistakes. You're never going to win the man and the mansion if you dress up like that and give him six hours of your time on the first date."

"No doubt your suggestion is that I spend more time with *you*."

"Or your parents or the dog catcher."

"Ultimately, what's in this for you?"

"That job I told you about. A nice, steady job with free housing."

"Judging by what you did to Lorrie today, I don't think he's going to want to hire you. Besides, how could you run the place? You're a rotten gardener."

"I can boss people around and I'm great with numbers. Give me some numbers to add."

"Thirty-nine, forty-two, eighty-one, two thousand and six, and seventy," she said quickly.

"Two thousand two hundred and thirty-eight," he answered instantly. "Comes in handy in business."

Holly gave a sigh. "I want to register here and now that I don't believe one word of your reasons for doing whatever it is you're trying to do. It's just that I can't figure out what you're up to. Yet. However, there is some wisdom in what you're saying. Today, Lorrie seemed a bit, well, a bit bored."

"By you?! He certainly doesn't know you like I do, does he? I bet if he saw you bare chested and in a concrete pit he wouldn't find you boring."

In spite of her intentions, Holly smiled. "I guess not." She held out her skirt, then the long, lacy sleeve of her blouse. "Taylor dressed me. She said that this outfit of hers was guaranteed to catch a man."

"She's right," Nick said solemnly. "She wore it and she caught Charles."

Holly shook her head at him. "You are truly wicked. Do you think we could get something to eat? I'm starving."

"Cucumber sandwiches for lunch?"

"And pimento cheese on tiny crackers."

Smiling, Nick kicked the motorcycle to life, but Holly couldn't figure out how to straddle the back. Should she pull her dress up to her hips? Before she could make a decision, Nick reached over and tore the side seam of the skirt from her midthigh all the way down to the hem.

At first Holly was shocked, then she laughed. At least she'd never have to wear the awful outfit again. She threw a leg over the back of the motorcycle, wrapped her arms around Nick's back, and they roared off.

# Chapter Fifteen

"TAYLOR," LORRIE SAID INTO HIS CELL PHONE, "I know everyone wants me to make mad, passionate love to Holly and to marry her, but she has to be the most boring person I have ever met." He paused. "Yes, she is very pretty. Beautiful even, and that body of hers is perfect, but she looks at me with great cow eyes and her lashes fan the breeze. I thought I might be sick."

Pausing, he listened to Taylor's ranting, to her threats, to her warnings.

Lorrie yawned. "By the way, exactly who is this gardener? The one with the motorcycle? I swear, when he rode up, *I* wanted to leave with him. No, of course I didn't let Holly know that. Tell me, dear, is Holly a virgin? She certainly acts like one. And dresses like one."

He paused. *"You* put her in that getup? Taylor darling, why don't you let her borrow your little black leather number, the

---

one with the spiked dog collar? Or is Charles wearing it *all* the time now?" He laughed at Taylor's answer.

"By the way, dear, young Holly said something interesting. She said the Belle Chere treasure was real. Yes, I know that it's just a family legend, and I know I was to tell the story just to interest Miss Hollander Tools, but she said Nick—that is the gardener's name, isn't it?—said the treasure was real. She was so positive when she said it that it made me think they'd found something in the papers in the attic. Has she said anything to you? No? Then perhaps it's wishful thinking on my part. I'm sure that if there were any treasure at Belle Chere my late father would have found it and used it to buy an underground mountain, or whatever real estate he could lose money on."

Lorrie waited. "Okay, I promise. I'll drag myself out of bed in the morning. She invited herself here for breakfast so I'll buy eggs—a lot of eggs. She has an appetite like a field hand. Should I make grits, too? Now, now, dear, no need for language like that. Who knows if Daddy is listening or not? And, by the way, couldn't we reconsider this marriage idea? You should have seen her today. If I'd said another sad word about my ex-wife or the state of my home, she would have whipped out her checkbook. Maybe—"

He listened to Taylor while looking at his nails, then smoothing his hair. "All right, dear, I understand. We need to be protected by the sanctity of the marriage contract. So be it.

Now let me go. I have some people to meet tonight. Yes, it is a private party. Very, very private, and, yes, they are trustworthy. Don't you have something to go to with Charles tonight? My, my, Taylor, such language. Your rich little baby sister would be shocked."

Smiling, he hung up.

# Chapter Sixteen

*One Month Later*

Holly and Nick were sitting on the floor of
the attic of Belle Chere. The big window fan was on and there
were three more fans sitting on the floor, but the room was
still hot. She was wearing a tiny pair of cotton shorts and a
halter top, while Nick had on just shorts.

Between the heat, the humidity, and her exhaustion, it was
all she could do to stay awake. For the last four weeks, she'd
had no rest. It was as though she'd become the rope in a
game of tug-of-war between two men. Lorrie took her days;
Nick took her nights.

Just in the past week she'd been to two dinner parties, a
country club dance, a swimming party, a picnic for a hundred,
and a flower show, all with Lorrie. Since the six-hour first
date, as Nick called it, she'd spent almost no time alone with

Lorrie. Instead, they'd entered into a mad social whirl in Edenton, Elizabeth City, and Windsor. Lorrie knew everyone and was invited everywhere.

True, she'd enjoyed herself–to a point. She'd laughed and talked and eaten well. But every evening, as Lorrie drove her back to Spring Hill, she'd been so tired she could hardly sit up. What was it about all that chatting that drained the energy out of her?

When they arrived at Spring Hill, Lorrie and she had been alone in his car and there had been time for good night kisses. But every time Lorrie made a move toward her, Holly had turned away–or yawned, or done something to keep him from kissing her.

"My little virgin princess," be began calling her.

At first, Holly had taken offense at the name, but as the days went by and the name kept Lorrie away from her, she began to like it.

But for all her fatigue, once she was out of his car, energy returned to her. Every night, without exception, she ran through her parents' dark garden to Nick's house.

He greeted her with open arms, never with questions or recriminations. They made love as soon as they saw each other, sometimes in the garden, sometimes in the house. It never mattered where, and each night their passion was renewed, never growing stale or slacking off.

After their first lust was quenched, they often took a

shower together, then they settled down to look at what Nick had found out that day. From the first day, Holly had made a stand: If she was going to go out with Lorrie to every social event within a hundred miles, then Nick was to be allowed to research at Belle Chere—and her father was to give him a fifty percent raise. That the money was Holly's was something that Nick didn't need to know.

Every night, their bodies damp from their showers and momentarily sated from their lovemaking, they shared a bottle of wine and went over whatever Nick had been able to uncover that day.

How Holly envied him! All day long she'd had to make small talk about her father's illustrious career, about the celebrities she'd met—and last, but certainly not least, about Hollander Tools. The people were always polite, but they asked endless questions about her and Hollander Tools.

All her life, Holly had worked to escape the stigma attached to being an heiress, but when she went places with Lorrie she had to smile at all the questions. She often wondered how much Nick knew about "who" she was, but if he did know, he never mentioned it.

As the days went by, the double life threatened to break her. During the day she was with Lorrie, the man she'd spent years fantasizing about. No boyfriend had ever come close to being as good as what she remembered about Lorrie. She'd dumped one man after three dates because she couldn't bear his laugh. She remembered Lorrie's laugh as being rich and deep, and, by comparison, the man's was too high.

But now she was an adult and she saw things as an adult. She now knew with certainty that she did not want to marry Lorrie Beaumont.

In that summer long ago she'd believed that Lorrie was like her. They'd spent the whole time in isolation and they'd worked long hours on restoring Belle Chere, and she'd enjoyed it so much that it had set the course for her future. It was that summer that she'd found what she wanted to do with her life.

"Tired?" Nick asked.

She opened her eyes and smiled at him. Her happy memories of time with Lorrie had been replaced with happy memories of time spent with Nick. In the evenings they'd pored over his photocopies of Belle Chere documents. He'd used his first week's salary to buy a copier and had carried it upstairs to the attic. (Lorrie had been willing to allow Holly to remove papers, but the only way he'd allow Nick to touch them was if they remained in the attic.)

Nick had done an excellent job of researching, finding all he could on the lives of the Beaumonts in 1842. He'd even found photos. They'd laughed at ugly little Arthur, and Holly had pretended to swoon over Jason's handsomeness. Julia had been sweet-looking, but even at sixteen, when the photo was taken, her eyes had been melancholy.

Teasing, Nick had made Holly pay in kisses to get to see

the photo of Julia's son. He'd looked exactly like his father, had been in the state legislature, and had six children, all of whom lived to adulthood.

For all Nick's research, they could find no mention of the treasure, and nothing in the private papers about Jason's trial or the hanging. There were boxes of documents left by Jason's son, but there was never a mention of his father or Arthur, who his mother had married. But then both men had died before the child was born.

After a week of nonstop socializing with Lorrie and nights spent with Nick, Holly was exhausted. But worse than the exhaustion was her inner turmoil.

She'd had two fights with Taylor just in the last week.

"Lorrie really, really likes you," Taylor had said with enthusiasm.

"That's nice," Holly answered. The night before, she and Nick had made love, read and talked, then made love again. She'd not gone to sleep until 3:00 A.M.

"You don't seem too happy about this," Taylor said, her voice rising.

"I'm just tired, that's all."

"Maybe we could make it a double wedding," Taylor said as though it was her dearest wish in the world to be married beside Holly.

"I don't think so," Holly answered, coming awake. "Lorrie and I—I mean, we don't—"

What had followed was one of Taylor's "big sister" lectures about marriage. She said that too many young girls didn't have the sense to look at the whole picture. They wanted some "hot" guy "like the gardener, Nick, for example," she'd said. Taylor had ranted for twenty minutes while Holly toyed with a bowl of cereal.

Before she'd come to Spring Hill, Holly thought exactly like Taylor did, that marriage was a business, a partnership. She'd fantasized hard about her life with Lorrie at Belle Chere.

It was just that the reality wasn't living up to the fantasy. First of all, Lorrie no longer seemed to be obsessed with the restoration of his ancestral home. She'd asked him about that and he'd given her a sly look and said, "I'll leave that to you."

Holly had looked away. It was clear that he meant when they were married. In an instant, her dream crumpled. She'd spent years imagining living at Belle Chere with Lorrie and how they'd work together to restore the plantation.

It had taken only a couple of weeks to realize that the Lorrie she'd seen that summer had been an anomaly. A fluke. A person who was not the real Lorrie. The real Lorrie liked going from one party to another. He said it gathered clients for his new law office, but, as far as Holly could tell, he never went to work.

As the days went by, Holly began to feel that Lorrie wanted her for something other than herself. Her inheritance, maybe? More than once he'd commented that he wished he could invite people to Belle Chere. "A beautiful Belle Chere," he'd said.

Holly had said nothing. Yes, she'd love to restore Belle Chere to what it once was, but then she wanted to do more with her life–and her money–than just entertain people.

"You're certainly not here today," Nick said, bringing her back to the present. "Want to tell me what's wrong?"

"Last night Lorrie asked me to marry him."

Nick was silent for a moment, then calmly said, "Congratulations. Tell me, is he a great lover?"

"The best," she said, then when Nick looked shocked, she grimaced. "You know very well that I've never been to bed with him. He calls me his 'virgin princess.' "

"Is that so?" Nick asked, smiling.

"I don't think any of this is funny."

"Me, neither," he said, smiling more broadly. "You know, if you don't marry him, you could always marry me."

"I really don't appreciate your jokes. Did you read all those letters in that pile or just some of them?" She tried to ignore Nick's eyes, but couldn't. She turned away, tears in her own eyes. "Nick, don't do this to me."

"Don't make you choose me over your family?" he asked softly.

She looked at him sharply, astonished by his insight. "I don't mean to hurt you. You're a wonderful man. No, you're too wonderful, but it wouldn't work between us. Short term yes, long term, no."

"Because of money," he said softly.

"No! Because of your pride. You want to live off of *me?* You want *me* to buy us a house and cars? You want *me* to pay to send our kids to private schools?"

She put her hands over her face for a moment, then looked back at him. "I've seen this happen over and over and it never works. Never!"

"You're talking about the class system."

"No, of course not. I mean, yes! My stepmother, Marguerite, ran off with a man like—I mean—"

"You mean with a man like me. Motorcycles and high school educations. We might throw our feet on the dinner table and pick our toenails."

"You're being ridiculous," she said, gathering up old letters and returning them to a shoebox.

"So you're going to walk away from us, leave behind weeks of laughter and great sex?"

"Yes," she said. "I was a fool to get involved with you in the first place. And you were a bigger fool for coming after me."

"I beg your forgiveness. Maybe you're more worldly than I am, but I'd never met a woman who I could talk with, laugh with, tell my secrets to, and make love to with such gusto. I couldn't let you go. I wanted to see if we were real. I needed to know!"

"And?" she asked softly.

When he looked at her, his eyes were hot, blazing with what he felt for her.

Part of Holly wanted to run away, but the larger part wanted to leap on him and say that she loved him, too.

Closing her eyes, she put her head back. Why had this happened to her? She didn't want to marry Lorrie only because she compared every move he made to Nick. Nick was quieter than Lorrie, more self-contained. Nick made people like him because he listened, and cared. The people around Lorrie looked at him with avaricious eyes. Lorrie owned a plantation that had been in his family for centuries. If there was an aristocracy in the U.S., Lorrie was part of it. But she'd never seen people really *like* Lorrie; they just wanted him because of who he was. Like they wanted to know Holly because of "who" she was.

But everyone liked Nick. Even her father liked him. Many times she'd seen the two of them in the garden talking. Once, Nick was deadheading roses while her father was asking his opinion on his latest sermon.

But it was one thing to like the man who lived in the servants' quarters and another to want your daughter to marry him.

When she looked back at Nick, his face had changed, shut down. Closed.

She wanted to argue with him until he saw reason, meaning that she wanted to make him agree with her. But what *did* she want? she asked herself. For them to part while tearfully smiling, no hard feelings, just a wise understanding between them? Did she think that someday they'd meet and introduce their spouses to each other? Maybe Nick's wife could work as a nanny to Holly's children?

She began to gather up the papers they'd gone through, but her eyes were so full of tears that she couldn't see. After a few moments she put her hands over her face and began to cry in earnest.

"Sssh," Nick said, gathering her into his arms and holding her. "Don't cry, sweetheart. I didn't mean to make you cry."

But Holly couldn't stop sobbing as all her frustration of the last weeks came out.

Nick recognized her need to cry. Later, he told himself. He'd tell her the truth about himself later and everything would be all right. True, she'd probably be angry, but she'd get over it, he thought.

Nick kissed her through her tears, and one thing led to another, and soon they were gently making love on the dusty attic floor.

"I love you," Nick whispered into her ear. "I love you to the height and breadth of an oak tree."

She held on to him, clung to him, but Holly still didn't stop crying. Somewhere deep inside her, she kept hearing, Last time. Last time. This was the last time they'd make love. With the words "marriage" and "love" having been spoken, things had changed between them. Irrevocably changed. They'd never be able to go back to where they had been.

They fell asleep in each other's arms, holding each other tenderly.

The fans whirled, sending cool breezes over their bare skin, and they slept as bonelessly as toddlers.

Neither of them heard the attic door open.

## Chapter Seventeen

LORRIE POURED A SCOTCH AND YET AGAIN CON-gratulated himself on his magnificence in handling Holly. He had spent four long weeks wining and dining her and introducing her to the right people.

It was a shame about her background, he thought. Her father's family was good, no property, no money, but good quality. However, her mother's family was little better than ... than that gardener Taylor lusted after, he thought, smiling. But then he'd done some lusting after that man, too. What was it about the lower classes in tight T-shirts with their great, roaring motorcycles?

He sipped his scotch and looked through the mail. Nothing but bills, all of which he threw in the trash. Soon he'd have a docile little wife to pay all the bills for him.

He ran his hand along a wall, felt the bulges in the plaster, and smiled. He'd renovate everything. From top to bottom he'd restore and renovate until Belle Chere was what it had once been. Soon the Beaumont name would be what it had once been, before men like his father had ruined it.

Smiling to himself, he walked into the living room and imagined silk curtains, brocade-covered sofas, an eighteenth-century armoire on the far wall. He imagined a white-coated servant serving him his icy scotch on a silver tray. A sterling silver tray. Monogrammed.

Yes, he thought, it was going to happen just as he and Taylor had planned it so long ago. That summer when he'd been just sixteen and hiding out from the world in embarrassment over his father's latest fraudulent land deal, Taylor had been twenty and as obsessed with her rich little stepsister then as now.

Taylor'd been so full of herself that summer; her beauty had been at its peak. She'd decided that she'd had enough of being second to Holly. "It's always the little heiress they want to meet," Taylor told Lorrie that summer. She'd hidden in the bushes and spied on Holly–something she'd done since her mother had married Holly's father–and seen them together.

From the first moment, Lorrie and Taylor had recognized each other as kindred souls. "So what do you want with her?" Taylor'd asked him. No introduction, just a blurting of those words.

Lorrie shrugged. "Free labor."

Taylor had nodded sagely and sat down by him. She told

him that she was planning to marry Charles Maitland. At sixteen, Lorrie had been shocked. "He's old and he's already married."

"He's rich and he has a pedigree, both of which I need."

Lorrie had laughed. He felt the same way. When there was something you needed, you went after it.

The summer had ended badly for Taylor because Charles had refused to divorce his ailing wife and marry the young, beautiful Taylor. "I'll get him," she'd told Lorrie. "If it takes the rest of my life, I'll get him back for the way he's treated me."

Lorrie hadn't heard any more from Taylor until many years later. By then his plan to get his hands on his wife's millions had failed. He'd managed to procure about two million from her without the ferocious men her first husband had left in charge of the money finding out, and Lorrie had invested it. His plan was to later go to her in triumph and show her what he'd done. If he stole and tripled the money it would be all right—and she'd give him more.

But Lorrie found out that he'd inherited his father's touch with investments. If he invested, the stock failed.

His wife's "overseers," as he called them, found out about the money and showed her. She divorced him in an instant. He'd begged and pleaded and made lots of promises, but to no avail. Years of Lorrie's drunken, all-night parties, plus the string of beautiful young men in the guest bedrooms, had made her deaf to his pleas.

During the divorce, Lorrie's law firm gave him notice. After all, his wife owned the firm, and she was the one who'd made sure her young husband was given credit for winning cases he'd never even worked on. It had been a matter of pride to her. To marry a young, beautiful man because he'd filled the empty place her husband's passing had created made her an object of ridicule. To marry a brilliant young lawyer was another matter.

In the midst of all this, Taylor had gone to Lorrie and made him a proposition. It seemed that Taylor regularly snooped in her stepsister's computer files, and she'd found out that Miss Hollander Tools had been carrying a torch for Lorrie for years.

In those same years, Taylor had been nurturing her hatred of Charles Maitland. She believed her life would have been different, better, if Charles had done what she wanted and married her. Over the years she'd blamed all her many failures on Charles and Holly.

"People expect me to do something," Taylor said. "They expect me to get a job." She shuddered delicately. "My mother says, 'Look at Holly. She's worth millions yet she works twenty-four/seven for state and national preservationist societies.'"

Taylor believed that if she'd been able to get her hands on Charles's money no one would have suggested she have a career. And if she'd been able to claim Charles's old-world name, she would finally outdo her stepsister. "Holly has money, but her mother was the lowest of the low. With Charles's money and his old name, I'd at last be able to win over her."

On that day when Taylor had reentered his life, she'd told Lorrie that Charles's wife had finally died so she, Taylor, meant to marry the man. "And make him regret turning me down the first time," she said, her knuckles white against her drink glass.

Together they came up with a plan that would solve all their problems. Taylor would marry Charles, and Lorrie would marry Hollander Tools—at least that's the way he saw it. As for Holly herself, he thought little. All he really cared about was Belle Chere, and Holly was eminently qualified to put glory back into his home.

"And then what?" Lorrie had asked idly. "Whatever do I do with a wife after the work is finished?"

"Kill her," Taylor said, making Lorrie pause, drink at his lips. "I'm her only heir now, but I'm sure her diligent firm of attorneys will immediately change her will once she marries you. You and I will jointly inherit."

"Murder?" he'd whispered. "I'm not sure . . ."

"If she died we'd split about two hundred million dollars."

After that statement, Lorrie had never looked back. He and Taylor had met in secret four times and worked on their plans. They'd thought of ways to kill Charles and Holly together, but Taylor said she wanted Charles to live so she could make his life as miserable as he'd made hers.

They connived and manipulated, with Taylor constantly dropping hints about Lorrie to Holly. "She thinks everything is her own idea."

"Does your mother?" Lorrie asked, curious.

Taylor's eyes slid to one side. "She . . . knows some of my true feelings for Holly, but I'm her daughter, so what can she do?"

During this time of planning, Lorrie had borrowed and begged money from every source he could. He had three mortgages on Belle Chere. He needed money to set up a fake law office in Edenton to impress Holly. He had to buy an expensive car and designer clothes. He had to look prosperous if he planned to court her. He couldn't look as though he *needed* her money!

While he was buying these things, he'd had to let Belle Chere rot. It hurt him to his heart to see the deterioration as he loved every inch of every blade of grass. But he needed to make Holly feel the urgent need for restoration. Urgency would make her marry him sooner.

Lorrie smiled. Last night he'd popped the question and even showed her a ring (not a real diamond, but she probably knew more about crescent wrenches than jewels), and she'd blushed rather prettily. She hadn't said yes yet, but he was sure she would. Afterward, he'd called Taylor in triumph. He assured her that there'd be a double wedding. It was a done deal. He'd invested everything and this time, he'd won! He was going to marry Belle Chere to Hollander Tools. Laughing at his own witticism, he stopped when he heard a noise upstairs. The gardener! That gorgeous hunk who worked for James Latham was upstairs nosing through Lorrie's personal documents.

Frowning, Lorrie mounted the stairs to the attic. At the top, he stood in the doorway and looked at Holly–innocent, virginal Holly–naked and wrapped around the equally naked body of the gardener.

In a flash, Lorrie saw the future. And he saw the past. He saw that for all his and Taylor's planning, Holly had gone her own way. She hadn't fallen for Lorrie; she'd reverted to her mother's base nature and run off with the gardener. Lorrie didn't know much about Holly, but he'd seen that she was– he hated the word–honorable. She was never tempted by party drugs or sexual suggestions. He'd thought she didn't even like to stay up late.

Now, looking at them entwined, and oh, so familiar with each other's bodies, he knew where Holly had been every night he'd dropped her off early.

But what Lorrie saw most was that he was in debt and there was going to be no rich wife to bail him out.

Taylor! he thought. All this was Taylor's fault and she was going to pay. She was going to do whatever needed to be done to get the money she owed him. She was going to get Charles to pay for the renovation of Belle Chere. Whatever, whoever, it didn't matter. Taylor was going to *pay!*

Turning, he went down the stairs to the entrance hall. On second thought, he went back to the library, reached behind a copy of Charles Dickens's *Oliver Twist,* and pushed a button. The bookcase swung open and revealed a shallow case full of rifles and pistols. He chose a 9mm, made sure it was loaded, then slipped it into his briefcase.

If verbal threats didn't work, maybe a gun would, he thought, as he left the house.

# Chapter Eighteen

HOLLY WAS THE FIRST TO AWAKE, AND FOR A LONG time she lay still, Nick's head on her shoulder, and caressed his hair. He'd become so familiar to her in the last weeks. She knew his every gesture, his every sound.

Visions of their time together over the last weeks flew through her mind—and all she seemed able to see was laughter.

Nick had asked her to marry him and she feared that if she did, the laughter would stop, and she couldn't bear that. She couldn't bear to see his eyes change from love to hatred.

Again, the words "last time" ran through her mind. She had an overwhelming feeling of sadness, a premonition that today was their last time together.

She kissed his hair and ran her hand across his bare back.

Nick shivered so violently he woke. Raising himself on his elbow, he looked at her. "I think someone just walked over my grave."

She smiled at him, caressed his cheek.

"Love me?" he whispered.

Holly opened her mouth to say yes, but she didn't because suddenly all hell broke loose. The blare of many police sirens seemed to surround them.

"Your father found out about us," Nick said.

Holly pushed him away. "Idiot," she said as she grabbed her clothes.

Pulling on his shorts, Nick went to the window. "There are six police cars," he said. "And a truck full of dogs."

Holly's eyes widened and in the next minute they ran down the stairs. By the time they reached the front door, the sheriff and three deputies were there. A dozen uniformed men and women were spreading out around Belle Chere, some with dogs on leashes.

"You're Miss Latham, aren't you?" the sheriff asked.

"Yes," she said hesitantly. "What—"

"Do you know the whereabouts of Laurence Beaumont?"

"Lorrie?" She put her hand to her throat and glanced at Nick, who stepped forward.

"We'd like to know what's going on."

The sheriff signaled for the two men behind him to step inside. "I have a search warrant for the house and grounds. We're going to need help. Do you know this place?" he asked Nick.

"I do," Holly said. "I can help you—" She stopped talking as a female deputy stepped from the back of a car, her eyes focused on Holly alone. "Miss Latham, I think you should go home immediately," the sheriff said solemnly.

Holly took a step backward and Nick put his arm protectively around her shoulders.

Over her head, Nick and the sheriff exchanged a look of understanding.

"I can show you around," Nick said. "I know the place pretty well, but give me a minute." He pulled Holly into the library and looked into her eyes. "I don't know what's happened, but I'm sure it's horrible and I can see that it involves you. Whatever it is, I want you to be brave. Can you do that for me?"

Holly nodded, but her heart was in her throat.

"I'll be with you as soon as I can, but for now I need to stay here and help." Smiling at her, his fingers found the chain of the necklace he'd given her and pulled it out of the inside of her top. Holding the big canary diamond to his lips, he kissed it. "For now I'll put my love in this. Keep it close to your heart always."

Holly's heart was pounding so hard she couldn't speak. In the hall the uniformed woman waited for her, waited with whatever terrible news that had made the sheriff tell Holly she needed to go home.

Nick kissed her forehead, then led her to the woman. He gave her fingertips one last squeeze, then she allowed herself to be led away.

When Holly was inside the car, Nick turned to the sheriff. "What happened?"

"Double murder. Taylor Latham and Charles Maitland were killed by Laurence Beaumont. He escaped and we're looking for him. Any ideas where he might hide?"

"I want protection put on Holly," Nick said.

"Think he might go after her, too?"

"She's worth a lot of money, I think he wanted it, and I think he realized he wasn't going to get it. I don't know what he might do."

The sheriff turned to a deputy and told him to put twenty-four hour surveillance on Miss Latham until Beaumont was caught. He turned to Nick. "You wanta tell me who you are?"

"Dr. Nicholas Taggert," he said. "Come with me and I'll show you where the firearms are kept. I discovered the cabinet by accident one day."

Longingly, Nick glanced out the open door. He wished he could be with Holly now, when she needed him, but in the last weeks he'd become very familiar with Belle Chere and he knew he'd be able to help the sheriff and his men search.

But luck wasn't with him. He didn't get away from the sheriff until late the next day. He'd had no sleep and little to eat while he trudged through swamps and across fields. He'd climbed through every building at Belle Chere, snaked under floors. Lorrie's scent was everywhere so the dogs smelled the man constantly. Whereas others took breaks, Nick didn't. He felt that Holly wouldn't be safe until Lorrie was in custody.

Finally, on the afternoon of the second day, Laurence Beaumont was found. He'd broken into the house of a friend who was away at the time. Lorrie had been living on canned beans and champagne, and when found, he told the sheriff's deputies that he was looking forward to prison food.

When Nick heard the news, he almost cried in relief. Holly was safe!

He was tired, dirty, unshaven, but he didn't waste time cleaning up. He jumped in Lorrie's rowboat and quickly rowed the short distance to Spring Hill.

He ran up the hill to the house and when he was within a hundred feet of it, he knew it was empty. He didn't bother to knock, but flung open the door and started running through the rooms. Upstairs, closets were empty.

He found Holly's room. Nearly all her belongings were gone. He picked up an earring from where it had fallen on the floor. It was a little ladybug and he'd seen her wear it a couple of times.

Clutching the earring in his closed fist, he went downstairs, then outside to his own house. As he knew there would be, there was an envelope on the little table in the kitchen.

He didn't want to open it, didn't want to see the words of farewell. After holding it a few minutes, he opened it.

My dearest Nick,

I'm sorry to end everything this way, but we are leaving. I have never seen my father so upset, and my stepmother is in a very bad way. She is being kept sedated.

I don't know where we're going, but I know we all need to be together now. Now we need to be a family and we need to try to heal.

Perhaps someday you and I–No! I can think of nothing but what's left of my family now.

As for Laurence Beaumont–I can no longer think of him as "Lorrie"–no one has any idea why he did what he did, nor do we care to know. He is a monster and deserves whatever horror happens to him!

I must go. I will miss you.

Holly

Nick held the note for quite a while. She hadn't told him she loved him, hadn't even signed the note "with love."

For a few minutes, he cursed himself. If he'd just told her the truth about himself, as he'd been warned to do, he'd probably be with her now.

He looked back at the note. She'd said that no one had any idea why Beaumont had killed Taylor and Charles and that she, Holly, didn't care to know.

"But I do," Nick said. "I want to know all of it."

# Chapter Nineteen

*Six Months Later*
*Christmas*

IT IS CHRISTMAS EVE, HOLLY THOUGHT, LOOKING around the bare rooms of Spring Hill and trying not to remember what had happened. The furniture had long ago been boxed and put into storage. For the last six months she'd been traveling in Europe with her parents, staying with one of her father's old friends after another.

For all her grief, Marguerite had been wonderful to Holly, introducing her to people and arranging parties for her. But every time Holly hinted that she'd like to return to the U.S., Marguerite became hysterical. It was as though, since she'd lost one child, she feared losing another one.

Her father had been stoical, showing great strength in helping his beloved wife, but, several times, Holly caught him looking at her. She could almost read his mind: What if it had been Holly instead of Taylor who'd been murdered by that madman?

Even though Holly said that she needed to get back to work, the truth was she was afraid to open a book. She was afraid of the solitude that reading required. If she had solitude, she was afraid she'd think, and that's what she didn't want to do. She didn't want to think about *why* Laurence Beaumont had murdered Taylor. Holly was afraid that if she thought about it, she'd see that, somehow, it was *her* fault. If she hadn't wanted Belle Chere so much, if she hadn't wanted to marry the owner, if she hadn't–

Holly walked away from the dining room windows. Returning to Spring Hill was worse than she'd thought it would be.

The truth was that guilt ate at her because what the house made her remember most was Nick. Not her sister, who'd been her best friend, but Nick.

For a moment Holly stood in the empty kitchen and looked out through the garden toward the caretaker's cottage–the house where Nick had lived. She was to sleep there tonight and she didn't know how she was going to be able to do it. How could she live with the memories of her and Nick that that house held?

Turning away from the window, she went into the living room.

For six months she'd returned to being a little girl and had allowed her father to deal with all the reporters and investigators. Holly had answered some questions, but she truthfully knew of no reason why Laurence Beaumont would kill Taylor and Charles Maitland. She knew of no connection among the three of them.

But no matter how she tried to avoid it, in odd moments, Holly had speculated. Had Taylor died because she'd been protecting her sister? Had Taylor found out what kind of man Laurence really was? Had she threatened to tell on him and that's why Taylor had been killed?

Every time Holly thought, she accepted another invitation. She didn't want time to think.

But, finally, the horror had caught up with them. Her father's attorneys had informed them that Holly was needed to testify at the trial. She had to tell what she knew about Laurence Beaumont III, who was claiming insanity as a defense. They were saying that because he'd shot Taylor and Charles in front of half a dozen witnesses, this was proof that he was insane.

"Like his ancestor," Holly's father said. "Like that Arthur Beaumont. Laurence Beaumont is a blood relative of that man and I should have realized when he told that story what he was capable of."

Neither Holly nor Marguerite had the energy to try to dissuade him of this absurd theory. Since neither James nor

Marguerite had spent much time with Laurence, it was Holly who was asked to return to the U.S. to testify.

On the plane back to the States, Holly tried to plan her testimony, but since she didn't know what she'd be asked she couldn't formulate her reply. She tried to read on the plane, tried to watch the movie, but she couldn't keep her mind on either of them. Nick, she kept thinking. Nick.

Where was he? What had happened to him?

Three weeks after they'd left, she'd casually asked her father what had happened to the gardener at Spring Hill.

"Quit or left, I don't know. I sent checks which he never cashed, but somebody else sent a bill for mowing so I guess it's being done. I put the house up for sale."

"Yes, of course," Holly had murmured and asked no more. As she'd always known he was, Nick had been temporary. He had been a guy to have a few weeks of great sex with, then discard. Nick Taggert was the type of man you have an affair with, but you married men like . . .

"Like Laurence Beaumont," she'd said aloud.

Somewhere in the six months they were away, Holly had seen what a mistake she'd made. She'd always thought that she judged people by what they were, not by their externals, yet, with nothing to base it on, she'd judged Nick to be. . . . Actually, she couldn't figure out what she'd decided he was, but she knew she'd misjudged him.

She kept remembering how he'd taken charge on the day

Taylor had been killed. He'd given Holly words of comfort even before he'd known what had happened. During the rest of that day and night and into the next morning, she'd heard repeatedly from the many law officials who wandered through their house that Nick Taggert was being a great help to them.

She'd wanted to stay and see Nick again, at least to say good-bye, but Marguerite had not been well. The doctor and her father had been insistent that they take her away as soon as possible.

In the end, all Holly could do was leave Nick a note and hope he'd understand.

She came back to the present and went upstairs. She had to see Taylor's room.

Her father's former assistant, a man who could arrange anything, had flown to Edenton to oversee the packing of the house. Part of Holly had wanted to do it, but she couldn't bring herself to say so. One look at the haunted eyes of her parents and she knew she couldn't leave them.

Taylor's bedroom was empty and had been freshly painted pink. The color made Holly smile. How Taylor would have hated it. Too frilly, too childish.

Sniffing, Holly straightened her back. She was done with tears. The new owners had a baby girl and Taylor's room was to be the nursery.

Holly went through the bathroom to her old bedroom

and, immediately, memories flooded her mind. Smiling, she remembered all the underwear she'd bought to wear for Nick, and how she'd hidden it away so Taylor wouldn't be jealous.

Jealous! Holly thought. Where had that come from? She'd hidden the underwear to keep Taylor from teasing her.

For a moment Holly put her hands to her temples. In the last six months, odd thoughts had run through her mind. She'd be dancing with some handsome young man and, suddenly, she'd look for Taylor's angry face, angry because she'd say that Holly was making a fool of herself again, that she was "showing off," trying to draw attention to herself.

Holly took a deep breath and tried to get control of herself. On occasion she hated herself because, sometimes, she felt as though her life was better now that Taylor was gone. A couple of times she'd thought that it hadn't been her father's disapproval that had made her run from Nick, but a fear of Taylor's sneers and put-downs.

Ridiculous! she'd told herself each time the thought crossed her mind. She'd broken off with Nick because she'd known it wouldn't work between them.

And it had broken up because Nick was so different from her. She'd always smiled whenever she thought that. "Different" was the last word to describe Nick Taggert. He'd helped her with her research. Every other boyfriend she'd had had complained that she spent too much time working. Only Nick had become involved with her work.

Even Lorrie, she thought, breaking her taboo against the nickname, had decreed that they not talk about her work, though her work was Belle Chere.

Holly looked out the window. She couldn't see it, but she knew that Belle Chere was through the trees.

And Belle Chere was to be sold at auction tomorrow, on Christmas Day.

It was true that Holly had returned to the U.S. to testify at the Beaumont trial, but that wasn't scheduled until the third of January. She would have stayed in Europe for Christmas, could have been with her family on Christmas Day, except for a letter sent from one of her father's attorneys.

In order to pay his legal fees, Laurence Beaumont was putting Belle Chere up for sale. Notices had been sent to preservationists and society people all over the world; a huge crowd was expected to attend the auction.

Holly had been eating breakfast when her father entered the room, the letter in his hand. She'd taken one look at him and known something was wrong.

Silently, he handed her the letter, then sat down.

She read it, and tossed it onto the table.

"I want you to buy the place," her father said.

"I don't want anything to do with anything that has the Beaumont name attached to it," she said.

When her father didn't reply, she looked at him and saw all the misery of the past months in his eyes. He'd aged horribly.

"I don't know that man well," he said and she knew he meant Lorrie, "but I do know that he loved that old house of his. His pride when he spoke of the place was as great a love as I've ever seen. No man has ever loved a woman as much as he loves that place."

Holly looked away, knowing her father was right, knowing that she'd been a fool to try to be part of that love.

"I want you to go there and buy that house. No matter what it costs, I want you to buy it, then I want you to restore it. For as long as that man lives he'll know that someone else is married to the woman he loves."

Holly hadn't liked what her father was saying, but she understood it—and she obeyed him. She'd flown into Dulles Airport in D.C. yesterday, rented a car, and driven down to Spring Hill this morning. She'd spend tonight in the caretaker's cottage and tomorrow she'd go to Belle Chere and outbid everyone. No matter how much it cost, she was going to buy it.

And after it was bought, she planned to never see it again. She'd hire people to restore it, hire people to live in it, or open it to the public. It didn't matter what happened, so long as she never had to see it again.

She looked at her watch. It was four o'clock and she was tired. She would go to the cottage, take a shower, eat the sandwich she'd bought, watch a little TV, then sleep. Yes, she thought, that's exactly what I'll do.

With resolve, she went downstairs, put the beautiful hooded

red cloak her father had given her, went out the front door and retrieved her sandwich and her suitcase from the trunk of the rental car. Yes, I'll just go to Nick's house and– Nick's house, she thought as she slammed the trunk lid.

In the next minute she'd tossed her handbag on the car seat and was driving away from Spring Hill–driving toward Belle Chere. Today was the open house so that prospective buyers and the curious could see the plantation.

She tried not to think during the short drive to the house. So many people were attending the open house that she had to park half a mile down the road and walk down the long, tree-lined drive.

She recognized some of the cars, and some had the name of their institutions painted on the doors, so she knew who was looking. She'd been right that every top museum in the U.S. would be there, and she knew that if one of them bought Belle Chere, it would be disassembled. The blacksmith shop would probably be set up on a lawn in Ohio; the dovecot would go to California; the smokehouse would go to Michigan. If the Metropolitan Museum of Art won Belle Chere, they'd probably take the dining room wallpaper back to New York to show in one of their display rooms.

As Holly walked down the drive, she saw a car with a discreet logo: JAMES RIVER. Even the Montgomerys were here, she thought. No doubt they'd disassemble Belle Chere to use at their beautiful James River mansions.

As she walked, she kept her eyes on the cars, refusing to look ahead to the house, afraid that it might cry out to her. "Save me," it would say. "Don't let anyone destroy me."

Holly refused to look up, but put her hands in her cloak pockets and raised the hood against the chill wind. Why had Lorrie chosen Christmas to do this? she wondered. Was it his sick humor to force all these people here on a holiday, a time when they wanted to be with their families? Lorrie was going to spend Christmas in a prison cell, so would he enjoy knowing that the people who coveted his house were as miserable as he was?

Holly nodded to a couple of museum people as they got into their cars, but they stayed away from her. There was no cheek kissing, no affectionate hellos. They knew what Laurence Beaumont had done to Holly's family, and they knew that in the competitive historical world Holly was a rival.

She managed to keep her eyes averted until she reached the front door of Belle Chere. It was ajar and she went inside. She wasn't surprised to see that the furniture was gone. No doubt it had been taken away to be sold separately.

Slowly, she began to walk about the house, and slowly, Belle Chere began to seep into her veins. She saw paneling that she had scraped clean then repainted. As she stood there in a semitrance, remembering, her old, false visions fell away and she began to really see the reality of that summer with

Lorrie. The truth was that they hadn't worked on the house together. The truth was that Holly had worked while Lorrie had watched.

She looked at the paneling in amazement. She'd seen what she'd wanted to see then and for many years afterward. Had she used Lorrie as an excuse? Had she wanted to break up with boyfriends and used her imagined "love" of Laurence Beaumont as an excuse to do it?

She walked through the downstairs rooms, remembering things he'd done that summer, but she was no longer seeing that time through a haze of lies. What was it Nick had said? That Lorrie had used her for child labor.

He did! she thought, and for some reason the knowledge made her smile. For the last six months she'd been in agony because she couldn't see how someone as noble and good as Lorrie had been able to commit murder.

"Still beautiful, isn't it?" asked a voice behind her.

Holly turned to see Nick standing there, and she nearly devoured him with her eyes. He looked great, a little thin maybe, but his blue eyes were still warm and laughing, and . . . cautious, she thought.

Instinctively, she took a step toward him, but halted when he didn't reach out to her. Okay, she thought, I deserve that.

"Yes, it's still beautiful." She wanted to say, So are you.

"How's your family?"

Holly waited until two men and a woman from a museum

in Dallas left the room. "Not well," she said softly. "They've taken it hard."

Nick nodded and waited for another person to leave. "Did they find out–" He cut off as two men entered the room and looked at Holly.

"Planning to open a factory here?" one of them asked snidely. "Hammers, maybe?"

"Better that than hanging polyester curtains," she said, smiling coldly at the man, referring to the tiny budget of his tiny museum.

Before the man could say anything else, Nick took Holly's arm and escorted her into the hallway.

"They're just looking," she said. "Half these people can't afford to buy Belle Chere. I don't know why they're here. They're just–" To her disbelief, tears rose in her eyes.

"Come on," Nick said, "let's go outside. The cold will feel good."

Nodding, she tried to get control of her emotions as they went down the stairs, passing five people on the way down. She couldn't help the anger that was rising in her. Belle Chere was one piece but she knew that these people, if they won it in the auction, would take it apart, break it up. They would–

"Better?" Nick asked once they were outside. It was sunny, but the air felt of snow, and Holly pulled her cloak tighter around her.

"A white Christmas," she said, breathing deeply. She could feel Nick looking at her, waiting for her to say something. "About that back there," she said at last. "That man meant . . . He said that about the hammers because . . ." She couldn't figure out how to explain.

"Because you're heir to Hollander Tools," Nick said softly.

"How long have you known?"

"Not until after we'd made love on about fifty things with 'Hollander' written on them."

"I see," she said, walking, looking ahead and not at him. "So you came here after you found out that I . . ."

"Yeah," Nick said. "I came here because I'd found out you were rich and I wanted your money."

She looked at him sharply, saw anger in his eyes. Smiling, she turned back and put her hands in her pockets. They passed two women and a man, who nodded at her.

"No," Holly said slowly, "you wanted my body."

"Still do," he said, and his words sent a little thrill up her spine. "If you've come to your senses, that is."

"Venice," she said, but didn't look at him. All the outbuildings were open for inspection and she was heading for the overseer's house. "I came to my senses in Venice. I was in a gondola with two beautiful young men and all I could think of was you."

"Yeah?" Nick said.

"Yeah."

He caught her arm and turned her to face him. He started to kiss her but stopped as two women walked past them.

It wasn't easy, but Holly pulled away from him. "Could we wait on this?" she asked softly. "I mean, could we postpone *us* for a couple of days? I have something to do for my father."

"To buy Belle Chere?"

"Yes," she said, "but how did you know?"

"It makes sense, considering what happened." He put his hand on her arm. "I have a lot to tell you. I haven't stopped searching since you left and I found out some things."

"You found the treasure?" she asked, teasing.

"I haven't been researching Belle Chere. I was searching for the truth of what happened the day you left."

Frowning, Holly pulled away from him. "I don't want to hear it."

"But–"

"Does what you found out disparage my sister in any way?"

"Yes," Nick said quietly.

Holly turned on her heels and started walking.

"Okay," Nick said from beside her. "So maybe I'll just talk about how much I love you."

"Not now," Holly said. "Not yet. I have to go to court in two weeks and–" She looked away.

They stood in silence for a few moments as two men came out of the overseer's house and looked at her with fallen faces. "Are *you* going to bid?"

"No," Holly said firmly. "I'm going to *buy*."

The men left and she went into the house, Nick behind her. "Do you think it was wise to say that?" he asked. "Maybe you should have sent an agent to buy the place for you."

She turned on him. "I want Laurence Beaumont to know that I bought what he loves so much. I want him to be in jail and read that I gave a fabulous party here, and that I'm enjoying what he wanted enough to kill for."

Nick raised one eyebrow at her. "Now that James Latham has spoken, could Holly come out and play?"

"I'd completely forgotten how infuriating you can be." She turned away and went into the sitting room.

There was a pretty, young African-American woman there who was, one by one, pressing every carved leaf that went across the mantel. It was an intricate carving of English ivy that twisted and turned and trailed down the sides. The carving had always fascinated Holly and she'd been told that it was the work of a slave who'd once been the overseer of all Belle Chere. "Before the war," Lorrie had told her.

Suddenly, Holly thought, For a slave to have been made overseer, he must have been a trusted servant. Very trusted. And smack in the middle of the mantel was carved the date, 1839.

"Oh!" the woman said, at last seeing that she was being watched. She jumped back guiltily. "I was, uh, I was . . ." Looking embarrassed, she picked up her handbag off the floor and started for the door.

"I'm Holly Latham," Holly said loudly, and the woman halted and turned back.

"I'm sorry about your sister," she said, taking a step forward. "I'm Kera Ivy. I teach at the local elementary and I thought I'd look around before someone buys the place and does whatever to it. I've always wanted to see the place and I thought that this would be my one and only chance."

The woman was talking too fast and too nervously. Holly figured her nervousness could be from several things, but she guessed that Miss Ivy had been doing something she wasn't supposed to be doing. It couldn't have been thievery. How could she have thought to walk through a crowd carrying a fireplace mantel? "What were you doing?" Holly asked.

"I, uh–" She looked at the tip of her shoe.

Nick stepped forward. "I'm Nicholas Taggert," he said, extending his hand.

"Oh!" she said as she shook his hand. "Are you one of these Montgomery-Taggerts? I read in the newspaper that they were going to be here."

"Yes, I am," Nick said, smiling. "My cousin wants to buy Belle Chere. Or maybe *I* will." He kept his eyes focused on Kera's, ignoring Holly's glare.

"Wow," Kera said. "Hollander Tools and the Montgomery-Taggert megacorporation bidding against each other. That will be exciting. I won't want to miss that. I think I'd better go home now and rest up for that. See you tomorrow."

As she headed for the doorway, Nick caught her right arm and Holly her left.

"So what were you looking for, Miss Ivy?" Nick asked.

"Nothing," she said. "I just thought it was a beautiful fireplace, that's all. And what with its being covered in ivy and my name being Ivy, it interested me."

Nick smiled at her. "Now, why don't I think you're telling the truth?"

"Because one liar can recognize another one," Holly said, giving him a false smile. "Because a low-down, slimy, sneaking rat can tell when someone else is up to no good."

Kera looked from one to the other and said, "I think I'd better go now."

Neither Nick nor Holly released her arms, but they quit looking at each other and looked at Kera.

"You were looking for something, weren't you?" Nick said.

Kera sighed. "Okay, so I was. If you'll release me, I'll tell you."

"I have a Thermos of hot chocolate in my car," Nick said. "I don't know about anyone else, but my feet are freezing."

"Sounds good," Kera said and Nick released her to let her pass.

"Mine's the black car by the entrance."

Kera walked ahead, Nick and Holly side by side behind her. "Did you bring the Bentley or the Rolls?" Holly said through clenched teeth.

"The Jag," he said cheerfully. "Instead of bidding against each other, how about if one bids and we split the cost?"

"Own something with you?" Holly asked. "Not in this lifetime."

"But I thought–"

"What?" she said, halting and glaring at him. "That when I found out you had money, I'd throw my arms around your neck and agree to marry you?"

"Actually, yes."

"Think again," she said, walking and nodding toward two men from a university in Arkansas.

"Holly," Nick said, pleading. "I wanted a woman who loved me for myself, not for my money. You can understand that, can't you?"

"I understand that you put me through hell." She was walking faster, moving ahead of Kera; Nick stayed right beside her. "I understand that while I was pouring out my deepest secrets to you–secrets I'd never told anyone else–you were lying to me about the very essence of who you are. While I was being torn apart, you were enjoying your little game immensely."

"I never enjoyed myself for one minute," Nick said.

She turned on him. "Never enjoyed yourself?"

"I didn't mean it like that. I meant I didn't enjoy what I was doing to you."

"Which was?"

"Making you fall in love with the gardener?" he asked, eyebrows raised.

"Gardener! You don't deserve the title. You—"

"Is this the car?" Kera asked, stopping at a long black limousine.

"No, that one." Nick pointed toward an inexpensive black Jeep.

"Slumming?" Holly asked.

"Saving to buy you a multiacre wedding present," he said as he opened the car door.

Angrily, Holly got into the backseat while Kera and Nick took the two front seats. Minutes later, Holly had removed her cloak, and was sipping the hot chocolate Nick handed her and doing her best to listen to Kera's story and block from her mind what Nick had done to her.

Kera had grown up in an old house that was locally known as "Ivy House" because all four of its fireplaces were decorated with carved ivy vines.

"I was told that before the Civil War, they were carved by my ancestor, who was a slave at Belle Chere. The two mantels upstairs are rather crudely carved, but by the time he got to the living room and the fourth mantel, the carving's good."

"So why were you pressing the leaves on the fireplace?" Nick asked.

"All four mantels at home have a secret compartment. You

press a leaf and a panel clicks down and reveals a little hiding place."

"How big?" Holly asked.

"The one in my bedroom can hold one Barbie doll snugly," Kera said.

"Unfair analogy," Nick said.

"You can talk of fairness?" Holly hissed at him. "You don't understand the concept." She looked back at Kera. "You think the same man carved the mantel in the overseer's house?"

"It looks the same to me. My great-granny said that our four were practice work for the real one, which she always told me was at Belle Chere. But since nobody local was ever invited to visit this place—unless we worked here, that is," she said bitterly, "I'd never seen the inside. When I heard of the open house, I thought I'd look for an ivy mantel. I stupidly assumed it would be in the big house."

Holly leaned back against the seat and thought. The dates were right. The mantel had been carved a few years before Jason Beaumont was said to have cleaned out Belle Chere, and the legend was that a "trusted servant" had helped Jason.

"Do you know anything about the man who did the carving? How he died and when?"

"Nothing. I've often wondered about him, though. If he was a slave, how did he come to own a house that's ten miles away from Belle Chere?"

"Maybe he carved the mantels and sold them and whoever

built the house bought them," Holly said. "How did your family come to own the house?"

Kera finished her chocolate and smiled. "Promise you won't laugh?"

"I believe I can promise you that for sure," Nick said.

"My great-granny used to tell me some tall tales that I loved to hear. She had to whisper them because my mother got angry. Anyway, Granny told me that my great-great-whatever-grandmother had purchased the house after the war with an emerald bracelet that had been hidden in one of the mantels."

She looked from Nick to Holly, who weren't smiling. "Silly, huh? Unless she stole the bracelet, of course, but, then she wouldn't have got away with it. Someone would have missed it."

"Not if the bracelet had been stolen and hidden some twenty years before," Holly said.

"Arthur, who would have prosecuted her, was dead by then," Nick said.

"And it was twenty years later, so Julia was probably dead, too."

"Who are Arthur and Julia?" Kera asked, then looked at her watch. "I have to go. I have a husband and kids who will starve if I'm not there to feed them."

"Maybe in a day or two we could visit your house, see the mantels, and tell you a story?" Nick said.

"Love to hear it," Kera said as she opened the car door and stepped out. "Ask anybody where the Ivy House is and they'll tell you."

They all said good-bye, then Nick and Holly sat in silence for a moment.

"Holly, baby–" Nick began.

She looked out the side window. "He–the faithful servant– helped Jason take away the wealth, including family jewelry, and they hid it together. Then Jason voluntarily went back to jail where he knew he'd be unjustly hanged."

"And the faithful servant was given an emerald bracelet as thanks," Nick said.

"He hid the bracelet in one of the mantels he carved," Holly said. "Probably inside the crudest one, the one no one would want so there was no danger they'd be used in the white man's fine house."

"The mantels and the bracelet were kept hidden for over twenty years, until the war was over and whoever owned the mantels was given freedom."

"But not him," Holly said. "It wasn't the man who stole the goods because I think he was supposed to tell Julia where the treasure was after Arthur was dead. I think he killed Arthur."

Nick looked at her. "Julia could have hidden a murder of Arthur. She had enough influence to get a doctor to say his death was an accident. And besides, the locals probably guessed what Arthur had been to his brother."

"And the faithful servant? Did he die with the secret of the whereabouts to the treasure?"

"That would be my guess," Nick said, then looked at Holly. "One Barbie doll isn't very big. What if he put the bracelet in one mantel and a map in another one?"

Holly's eyes widened. "If he was the overseer, he'd want the map where he could keep a close watch on it, say, maybe over his own fireplace."

"And if he'd made four practice mantels, by the fifth one he'd have come up with a pretty ingenious way to hide the opening, one that a little girl couldn't find."

For a moment Nick and Holly stared at each other, then she turned away. "When I own this place, I'll start searching," she said.

"Right. If you started searching now it would be illegal. Now it's still owned by Beaumont."

"Yes," Holly said. "I'll be here for the auction tomorrow, buy the place, wire the money here, wait for the attorneys to do the paperwork, then I'll see if there's a secret compartment, if there's anything in it, then wait until after the snow melts so we can see where to dig, maybe even wait until after winter, and if it's there I'll find it. It will be a fitting end to my dissertation."

"Perfect," Nick said. He was leaning back in the driver's seat and staring out the window. "All legal and sensible."

"Yes," Holly said from the back of the seat. "Legal and sensible."

"Besides, they've stationed armed guards to patrol this place since . . . well, since the tragedy. Lots of curiosity seekers around here. We'll just wait and do it all when it's safe and legal."

"Right," Holly said. "Safe and legal."

They were silent for several long moments, then Holly said, "Greenville."

"Right," Nick said as he started the car and Holly climbed through to the front seat. As Nick pulled out into the driveway, he said, "Lowe's, right?"

"Or Home Depot." She opened the glove box. "So where's something I can make a list on?"

He opened the compartment in the console and she took out a pen and a notebook and began to write. "Flashlights, shovels, rope."

"Saw," Nick said. "By the way, do you get a discount if we buy Hollander tools?"

"*You* pay double," she said sweetly.

# Chapter Twenty

"I'm hungry," Holly said, holding her cloak close to her. "I wish we'd stopped to get some sandwiches."

"We'll take whatever we find to the nearest restaurant where there are lots of lights."

"And to a twenty-four-hour copy place."

When he took her arm as she stepped over a rough place in the plowed field that bordered Belle Chere's land, Holly jerked out of his grasp and nearly fell. "I haven't forgiven you," she said.

"Oh, right, I forgot. How long do you think it will take?"

"Longer than you have years left."

Nick chuckled as he shifted the big bag on his shoulder. It was full of black-out fabric that they planned to use to cover the windows in the overseer's house while they searched, and several tools, all of them stamped with the Hollander name.

"Remember," Holly said, "that no matter what we find, we

don't search for anything until after the auction, until after I own Belle Chere."

"About the auction . . ." Nick said. "Maybe I should buy the place and put it in my name."

Instantly, Holly halted, then turned on her heels as though she was planning to go back.

"Okay," Nick said. "You win. You buy it."

In the next second, they turned off their flashlights and fell to their stomachs in the dirt as a guard carrying a huge flashlight went by. Once he was out of sight, Nick stood and signaled for Holly to follow him. Under cover of darkness, they ran to the overseer's house.

It was locked. Nick pulled bolt cutters out of the bag, but they would only cut the latch–the old handmade, wrought-iron latch. Holly shook her head vigorously, then motioned for Nick to follow her.

Smiling in triumph, she pointed to a window that, earlier, she'd opened a couple of inches. The problem was that the overseer's house, like all the buildings at Belle Chere, was set on brick pillars, which made the window high above their heads.

Silently, Nick cupped his hands for Holly to put her foot in them, but as soon as she was halfway up, he opened his hands so that she fell, her body sliding against his all the way down.

"Stop it!" she hissed in his ear when he began to kiss her neck.

Think of Taylor, she thought, and pushed away from him. For a moment she wondered what some wild-goose chase for some probably nonexistent treasure had to do with her sister's murder, but she erased that from her mind. She again stepped into Nick's hands and pushed herself up.

As she knew it would, the window opened easily (when she was thirteen she'd painted herself into a corner and had had to escape out that window). Tossing her cloak onto the floor, she went in after it, head first.

After Nick tossed her the big bag, for a few seconds she was tempted to not help him get into the building. But she thought he might have some ideas of where to look, so when he jumped up and caught the ledge, she helped pull him in. Silently, they thumbtacked the black cloth over the two windows in the room, and around the door. They wanted no one to see their light. When they'd finished, they turned on the big flashlights they'd bought and aimed them at the carved mantel.

An hour later, they'd pushed and wiggled every carved leaf, but with no results.

They sat down, wrapped Holly's cloak around them, leaned against the far wall, and shared a bottle of water.

"Where would *I* have put a secret compartment?" Nick whispered.

"You would know, since secrets are your life."

"You didn't tell me you were heir to Hollander Tools," he said, "so you had a few secrets of your own."

"I had one; you had a thousand. What was all that you told me about your life, about how you didn't have a TV until you were nine?"

"It's true. We had every video my mother approved of, but she hated what was being shown on TV."

"That's quite different from the way you presented your childhood to me. I guess the house so many of you lived in together and that 'constantly needs repair' is that marble mansion in Colorado."

"The very one." During this exchange Nick didn't look at her, but just kept staring at the mantel. "Where would *I* put a compartment?"

"If it were me, I wouldn't make a little flip-down door. It's too easy for things to get stuck inside and too hard to get them out. I'd make an old-fashioned drawer, one that no one's likely to accidently open by leaning against it."

They looked at each other with wide eyes, and in the next minute they were back at the mantel, this time pulling instead of pushing.

Holly found the drawer. It was so tightly wedged in place that it took them three tries to get it out. When they did, they saw a roll of cloth inside. Their breaths held, they removed the cloth and untied it. Inside was a piece of parchment, old and brittle.

Slowly, they unrolled the paper on the floor in front of the light.

It was a simple and crudely drawn map, made by a person with little education. A dotted line ran from the main house of Belle Chere, past the slave quarters, past the stables, followed the river, then ran into the swampland. At the end was a drawing of a tree shaped like a Y.

"What's this?" Nick asked, pointing at a symbol in the corner.

"It's a sword," Holly said softly. "It's an old sword that a tree has grown around." She looked at him. "All this time I've known where the treasure was."

"You ready to go?" Nick asked.

"Now? It's pitch black out there," Holly said.

"Does that mean you can't find the place?"

"Blindfolded."

Nick gave her a look to say, So?

Holly grimaced. "You never let me sleep."

Nick offered her his hand to pull her up. He started to kiss her, but she turned her head away.

"Just remember that the auction is at nine A.M. tomorrow and I plan to be there," she said.

Chuckling, Nick gathered their belongings and put them in the bag. They carefully and reverently returned the map to the drawer, and left the cloth over the windows and doors.

"I'll own Belle Chere by this time tomorrow and I'll take it down then," Holly said, fastening her cloak about her neck.

Nick climbed out the window first, caught the bag Holly

handed him, then helped her climb out. It was as though he had a hundred hands, all of which he ran over her body.

When she reached the ground, she tried to glare at him, but she couldn't quite pull it off. The truth was, she had to work hard to keep from grabbing his shirt and tearing it open.

"I've missed you so much," Nick whispered.

If the flashlight of the guard hadn't come close to them, Holly was sure they would have ended up on the ground together.

They scurried around to the front of the cabin, out of the beam of light, then, crouching, they ran into the trees.

Because of the dark, because they were afraid of being seen, they didn't turn on their lights. Instead, Nick followed Holly, often stumbling into the back of her, then grabbing her with his hands to keep from falling. However, his hands always seemed to land on her breast or hips or around her thighs.

"Would you stop it!" She knew her attempt to sound indignant was less than successful. She wondered what in the world she was doing outside in the middle of the night. The temperature was dropping and the air felt heavy; snow was imminent.

"Maybe we should go back," she said. "Maybe–"

"Someday we'll tell our kids about this. We'll say, 'Remember the day we spent Christmas Eve looking for treasure?' It'll become folklore in our family."

"Maybe I'll tell *my* children," she said. "The ones I have with Prince Raine."

"Oh," he said. "Lanconia. Did you know that my middle name is Raine? It's a name that's been in our family for generations."

Holly grimaced, but she didn't let him see it. "Cousin?" she asked.

"Cousin."

So much for trying to make him jealous, she thought.

"Tell me about this tree," he said, looking back at Belle Chere. They were far enough away now not to be heard.

So many things had happened over the years that she hadn't thought of the tree in a long time. She'd first seen it when she was thirteen. She'd meant to ask Lorrie about it, but he'd been distracted that day and there always seemed to be other things to talk about.

She began to tell Nick the story as they made their way into the dark forest.

As she often had done when Lorrie wasn't there that summer, she'd taken a break from scraping paint and wandered around. There was a deep curve in the river that formed a teardrop of land. He'd told her that there was supposed to be an old Indian burial ground on that piece of land so she'd been curious. She'd battled her way through thorn bushes and grapevines to find an area that had little undergrowth. The tall trees shaded the ground so deeply that grass didn't grow, and under her feet was a soft padding of years of mulch.

She'd spent three hours walking through the heavily forested area, looking at the trees, listening, and one time sitting on a grapevine and swinging.

As she was about to leave, she noticed an enormous beech tree that split into two huge branches several feet up. There seemed to be something embedded in the tree right where it split.

After looking around to make sure Lorrie wasn't near, Holly used a nearby grapevine to hoist herself up into the tree. Since she wanted Lorrie to think she was all grown up, she didn't want him to see her climbing a tree like a child.

When she reached the object, she saw that it was the handle of what looked to be an old sword. It looked as though, many years ago, someone had tied a sword horizontally across the split in the tree and, gradually, the tree had grown around the sword until little of it could be seen.

"All these years and you'd think someone would have seen it, " Nick said.

"I'm sure they did, but since the legend of hidden treasure was kept quiet, no one was looking for a marker. Besides, a sword in a tree isn't unusual around here. By the stables is a tree with an old iron sticking out of it."

"Think it marks a pile of laundry that needs washing?"

"If so, then *you* buy the place."

Nick laughed.

Minutes later, they reached the tree and Nick shined his light up. There was little they could see, just an enormous tree with some knobby thing sticking out of the side of it. To see what it was they'd have to climb up.

Nick put his bag on the ground. "So now what do we do? Wait for morning and rent a backhoe?"

Holly walked around the tree. "How could anyone have planted a tree on top of a cave? Where would the roots grow?"

"Not dumb, are you?" he said, picking up the biggest flashlight and shining it at the roots. On three sides, the roots were easy to see as they spread out across the ground. On the fourth side, the roots were growing right and left, but not in the center.

"We're going to have smart kids," Nick said, grinning at her.

"You and your wife?" she asked innocently.

"Yes, my wife and me."

She couldn't help smiling. "Okay, John Henry, get the shovel and start digging."

"Since all these tools have your name on it, shouldn't you do the honors?"

"I found the tree," Holly said. "Besides, I'm sleepy. I think I'll–"

She broke off because, suddenly, the ground seemed to

give way under her. It was as though she'd stepped into quicksand and was going down.

"Nick!" she screamed.

He was on the other side of the tree, removing a shovel from the bag, but he turned and saw Holly sinking down. Dropping the shovel, he leaped, his arms outstretched. But he wasn't fast enough.

In seconds, where Holly had been standing was a hole.

Nick, on his belly, inched forward. "Holly," he called, fear in his voice. "Are you all right?" When she didn't answer, he inched backward, grabbed the flashlight, then crawled forward again and shined his light down.

Holly was about ten feet below him, her cloak splayed out around her. She was sprawled on top of what looked to be a pirate's treasure of silver ornaments, gold coins, and a few pieces of jewelry winking in the light.

Nick kept his eyes on Holly. "Are you all right? Holly, baby, honey, answer me. Look at me."

She didn't move, but she opened one eye. "Are there any rattlesnakes up there?"

"No," he said, so relieved he was near tears. "Unless you count me. Holly, honey, I haven't told you this, but I'm actually a doctor."

She opened both eyes in surprise. "A doctor?"

"Yes, so I want you to take off all your clothes, except for your shoes and your watch, and–"

"You idiot!" she said, laughing.

"It's just that I had such a very, very good time the last time you were naked and in a pit that I want to repeat the experience."

Gingerly, Holly tried to sit up.

"Careful," he said, "that stuff is hard."

"What stuff?" she asked, sitting up, rubbing her lower back. "I'm covered in bruises."

"I'll kiss each one to make it well."

"Is that what they taught you in medical school?"

"Sort of. Well, not *on* campus, but off–"

"I don't want to hear." Reaching behind her, she grabbed something and pulled it from under years of debris. She blinked at it a couple of times. It was black and had some kind of fungus on it, but it looked to be a candelabra. "Eighteenth century, I'd say. Probably English, but it could be French."

She lifted her left leg, reached under it, and pulled out something sharp that was sticking her. It was a ring. She rubbed it on her sleeve. "Look at this. I think I may have found the ring that matches the emerald bracelet." She lifted her right leg. "Wonder if the necklace is here? Or a tiara? I don't have a single tiara to my name."

"Now, isn't that a tragedy?" came a voice, and both Nick and Holly looked into the eyes of Laurence Beaumont the third. He was holding a flashlight and a gun.

# Chapter Twenty-one

Bᴇᴀᴜᴍᴏɴᴛ ᴀɪᴍᴇᴅ ᴛʜᴇ ɢᴜɴ ᴀᴛ Hᴏʟʟʏ's ʜᴇᴀᴅ ᴀɴᴅ said he'd kill her if Nick didn't get into the pit with her. Since Beaumont had nothing to lose, Nick had instantly jumped down into the pit beside Holly, fully expecting Beaumont to start shooting.

As Nick looked up from the pit at Beaumont as he hovered over them, Nick's only thought was to protect Holly. As far as he knew, he was the only person to know the full extent of Beaumont's insanity.

During the six months that Holly had been traveling with her family, Nick had been digging for information. He'd hired people to find out everything about Taylor Latham, Charles Maitland, and Laurence Beaumont.

Within weeks he'd dismissed Maitland as an innocent bystander, but Nick had been shocked at what he'd heard and read about Taylor and Beaumont. If it was weird and bizarre and bordered on the illegal, then those two were involved.

Nick read reports of bartenders who remembered seeing Beaumont and Taylor together in the months before Holly's father bought Spring Hill.

Nick knew that Holly believed she'd been the one to manipulate her entire family into moving next door to Belle Chere, but Nick saw that Holly had been the one who'd been maneuvered. And used, he thought.

Over the months, as the story began to unfold, Nick had pieced things together. Beaumont had planned to marry Holly for her money. As when she was a child, she would probably have been used as free labor to do all the work of restoration at Belle Chere, then she'd . . . what? Meet with an accident? Had that been the plan? Nick never doubted that kindhearted Holly would have left a will giving her fortune to her sister and her husband.

As for Taylor's marriage to Maitland, Nick figured it was a combination of social climbing and greed. Maitland was worth a couple million, nothing compared to Holly, but it was some. Nick guessed Taylor wanted Maitland's old-world name as much as anything. One report told how Taylor often spoke with hatred of her father's background.

Snobbery and greed, Nick thought. All of it had been caused by snobbery and greed.

The only thing that puzzled Nick was why Beaumont had killed Taylor. What had gone wrong?

"How'd you manage to escape?" Nick asked, putting himself between the gun and Holly.

Beaumont smiled. "Call it a family trait. I sold"–he swallowed–"my furniture and used the money to grease some very dirty palms."

He pointed the gun at Holly, nearly hidden behind Nick. "I should have killed you two, you know, but Taylor made me so very angry that all I could think of was getting *her.*"

Holly was trying to get in front of Nick, but he wouldn't let her.

"What did she do to make you angry?" Nick asked.

"She laughed at me," Beaumont said, looking down at them. "Can you imagine that? *She* laughed at *me*. You see," he said slowly, "I told her about finding the two of you together in the attic. Taylor and I had laid such careful plans, but *you* stepped in and destroyed them. If it hadn't been for you, stupid little Holly would have married me. When she was thirteen she absolutely worshiped me."

"I did no such–" Holly began, but cut herself off when Nick put pressure on her arm.

"So you took a gun and went to visit Taylor."

"I only meant to frighten her, but she was at a party, having a wonderful time, while I was . . ."

"You were going through hell," Nick said, sounding sympathetic. He was moving one foot and Holly saw that he seemed to be trying to unearth something. Looking down, she saw what looked to be a knife, some souvenir from a trip to the Middle East by the look of its jeweled handle.

"Yes," Lorrie said. "I was in misery, but Taylor was laughing. She told me she had what she wanted, meaning Maitland's money and his name, so she didn't care about me. She didn't care that if I didn't get Hollander Tools I was going to lose my family home."

Suddenly Holly put her hands over her face and began to cry loudly, collapsing into a heap on the pile of goods.

Lorrie waved the gun. "Shut her up."

Nick patted Holly's head and took a step to one side, giving Holly better access to the knife by his foot. "And Belle Chere is everything to you, isn't it?" Nick asked quietly.

"Of course," Lorrie said, standing up. "In order to keep the place, I was willing to marry *her.* Can you imagine? A tool manufacturer's granddaughter?" He shuttered delicately. "She's one generation away from being poor white trash. To think of someone like her being mistress of my home. Boggles, doesn't it?"

"Why are you here?" Nick asked. "Why aren't you on the run?"

"That was my plan, but I wanted, no I *needed,* one last look at . . ." He couldn't seem to say the name. "I saw you two skulking about in the dark. You know what I did? I crawled under the overseer's house so I could hear you. Me. *I* crawled. I lay in the dirt to listen to you two discussing who was going to own *my* home."

He paused as he seemed to need time to calm himself. "When I heard what you'd found I decided to follow you." He shined his flashlight around the treasure of Belle Chere. "So the legend was true. Auntie told me Arthur Beaumont sold all the house slaves down to Mississippi to work in the cotton fields to keep them from telling what Jason had done. You see, Beaumont pride is very important to us."

He glared at Holly. "But *you* have destroyed us."

Slowly, clinging to Nick, Holly stood up. Her body was so close to his that Lorrie didn't see her pass him the narrow-bladed dagger.

"What do you plan to do to us?" Holly asked.

"Why, kill you of course. Kill you and leave your bodies to rot. It will be years before anyone finds you."

"Do you know who my family is?" Nick asked quietly.

"Oh, yes. I found that out long ago. Did you know that that stupid little toolmaker's granddaughter has no idea what that yellow stone around her neck really is? She told Taylor she thought it would turn her neck green. Can you imagine that *I* was supposed to *marry* someone so low class?"

"If you kill me," Nick said, "my family won't let you get away." He kept his eyes on Lorrie, ignoring Holly's puzzled look, but he could feel her hand go to the necklace.

"If I lose Belle Chere, what does it matter if I live or not? Now which of you wants to die first?"

It was at that moment that Nick threw the knife and it

landed in the middle of Lorrie's throat. He staggered for a moment, then fell backward onto the ground above them.

It took Holly a moment to realize what had happened, then she collapsed into Nick's arms. He held her, and for the first time since Taylor's death, Holly really cried, not superficial tears full of guilt, but real tears, tears that released her.

Nick held her to him, stroked her hair, and kissed her tears. At about four, Holly fell asleep in his arms and the snow finally began. Holding Holly, he looked up through the hole at the big flakes drifting down to them. He wasn't worried about being found. When neither of them showed up for the auction, his family would call in helicopters and dogs. He had no doubt that his family would come for him.

Holly stirred in his arms and he kissed her soft lips.

"Forgive me?" he asked.

Opening her eyes, she nodded. A few hours ago she'd been at death's door. Holding onto her anger at a man she loved seemed frivolous.

"Merry Christmas, darling," he said.

"Merry Christmas," she replied, then kissed him in return.

They made love on top of the silver, the gold, and the jewels, with the snow falling down on them, not feeling the cold, feeling only their love for each other.

At eleven, they were sleeping under Holly's cloak and wrapped around each other to stay warm, when Nick's cousin Mike looked down on them.

"Hey!" Mike called down. "You two want to be rescued or you want to stay in there?"

"Is it clear up there?" Nick asked, feeling Holly begin to awaken.

"Yes," Mike said, knowing his young cousin was referring to the body of Laurence Beaumont. It had been removed.

"So who won Belle Chere?" Nick asked, feeling Holly's eyes on him.

"I did, but I'll sell it to you for a dollar."

"No," Nick said. "Give it to Miss Latham."

Holly squeezed Nick's hand, but said nothing. A few days ago she'd wanted nothing to do with a place associated with the Beaumonts, but now she thought that Belle Chere needed new blood. It needed a cleansing, a renewal.

A ladder was lowered for them and Holly went up first. As Mike Taggert helped her step onto solid ground, he said, "Nice necklace."

Behind her, Nick said, "I took your advice," and both men laughed.

"What was that all about?" Holly asked.

"Mike told me who I should give the necklace to and I obeyed him." He put his arm around her. "Come on, let's go see your Christmas present."

"Oh, no you don't," she said. "Not so fast." She held up the necklace to the sun. "What is this thing and how much is it worth?"

"It's a flawless canary diamond and it's worth a few mil. Come on, let's go."

She didn't move. "But what did you mean when you said you took Mike's advice?"

"He told me to only give it to the woman I planned to marry."

"But you gave me this necklace before you came to Edenton."

"You mean, *before* I knew I could win you away from another man?"

She nodded.

"I never had any doubt that I was going to win you. You were mine from the moment I looked down into that pit—the first one."

"But . . ." she began, but then she smiled. They'd have time to argue later. Now she wanted to walk with him and look at Belle Chere, the place that was to be their home.

That night they slept in a double sleeping bag on the floor of the overseer's cabin, a fire burning in the ivy fireplace.

"To the Holly and the ivy," Nick said, holding up a champagne glass in toast.

"This is the best Christmas of my life," Holly said. "It can't get better than this."

"Yes, it can."

"Oh," she said, looking down. "Taylor and Lorrie. And poor Charles Maitland."

"No," Nick said, looking at her with hot eyes. "Next Christmas we'll have a couple of kids."

"A couple!" she said, laughing. "What an ego you have."

"Did I tell you that twins run in my family?"

"There's a whole lot you didn't tell me about your family," she said, then smiled at him. "Do twins take more work to make than singletons?"

"I don't know." Nick seemed to think about the matter. "But if they do, we'd better get started." He moved toward her.

"I want a big tree," she said under his lips. "And we'll decorate it with fruit like they did when Belle Chere was built. And we'll–"

She didn't say any more.